"Would your equine therapy be open to me?"

Meredith nearly dropped her currycomb. Suddenly Jace's interest in observing her sessions made more sense. It wasn't about making sure the structure met her needs; it was about meeting his own.

"I don't think that's a good idea."

"Why not?" Jace asked.

Meredith wasn't used to serving adults in equine therapy, much less an attractive man who'd broken her friend's heart. But she couldn't deny there was something between Jace and Bella. Her mare had loosened the man's tongue out on the trail, and obviously, he needed more.

"With you building my arena, there's a huge conflict of interest. I can refer you—"

He shook his head. "No. No way."

Her heart sank and twisted. She was a sucker for someone who needed help. But there were ethics to follow in her line of work.

Meredith needed to put away her preconceived opinions of Jace Moore and hope that the attraction she felt for him would be extinguished, too. Her license and her very career depended on it.

Jenna Mindel lives in Northwest Lower Michigan with her husband and their dogs, where she enjoys the Great Lakes, the outdoors and strong coffee. Her love of fairy tales as a kid paved the way for creating her own happily-ever-after stories. She loves to write flawed characters who realize their need to trust God before they can trust each other. Contact Jenna through her website, www.jennamindel.com.

Books by Jenna Mindel

Love Inspired

Mending Fences
Season of Dreams
Courting Hope
Season of Redemption
The Deputy's New Family
Rebuilding His Trust

Second Chance Blessings

A Secret Christmas Family
The Nanny Next Door
Finding Their Way Back

Visit the Author Profile page at LoveInspired.com for more titles

REBUILDING
HIS TRUST

JENNA MINDEL

LOVE INSPIRED
INSPIRATIONAL ROMANCE

LOVE INSPIRED®
INSPIRATIONAL ROMANCE

ISBN-13: 978-1-335-23041-6

Rebuilding His Trust

Love Inspired
22 Adelaide St. West, 41st Floor
Toronto, Ontario M5H 4E3, Canada
www.LoveInspired.com

HarperCollins Publishers
Macken House, 39/40 Mayor Street Upper,
Dublin 1, D01 C9W8, Ireland
www.HarperCollins.com

Printed in U.S.A.

Recycling programs for this product may not exist in your area.

And now abideth faith, hope, charity, these three;
but the greatest of these is charity.
—*1 Corinthians* 13:13

I'd like to thank Courtney Sumpter, MS, OTR/L, and founder of Northern Michigan Equine Therapy, and Holly Henagan, LMT, for their time and willingness to share insight into the field of equine therapy. You ladies are amazing and I loved getting hands-on with one of your horses to walk through an exercise. Thank you for what you do!

I'd also like to thank my dear friends Jim and Teresa, for their wealth of knowledge about caring for horses. I've enjoyed lots of love and fun with the Yell horses over the years and I'm better for it. You guys are a blessing!

Chapter One

Meredith Lewis stepped outside as a navy pickup truck pulled into her driveway. She was finally going to meet the infamous Jace Moore, who'd broken her friend's heart. As the truck parked, she noted the logo with white lettering spelling out *Three Sons Construction* under three rooftops with a hammer crossing a ladder. Clean and clever.

Despite her reservations about the man who'd come to give her an estimate, she'd been told his company was good. Hopefully, Three Sons Construction could do what she needed done, and soon. Meredith had spent the better part of her summer looking for a contractor and had come up empty-handed. She had the funds and a folder full of ideas for an indoor riding arena with no one willing or able to do the work.

Her friend Liza had referred Three Sons Construction because the eldest Moore brother was a longtime member of Liza's church. Jace Moore had recently returned to said church, where he'd

Rebuilding His Trust

dated and then dumped her best friend. It'd be hard not to hold that against him, but regardless, Three Sons Construction was her last hope.

A tall, dark-haired man stepped out of the parked truck and as he walked toward her, Meredith couldn't help but stare. He had a lean build, yet she could easily see the strong muscles of his upper arms from here. Liza hadn't been kidding when she'd said Jace Moore was handsome. Really—very—handsome.

Nerves skittered up her spine, but it didn't matter what he looked like. Meredith wasn't interested in a guy who could callously discard the affection of someone as sweet as her friend. Jace Moore had a reputation that went with his looks, according to Liza, who'd grown up here in Rose River, Michigan. He was one of those guys who dated around.

Not that he'd even look my way. Guys like him never do.

Meredith shook off the disloyal thought. She didn't want him looking her way. She didn't want anything to do with the man other than an estimate. Hopefully, the brothers would build the arena she needed in order for her business to grow. To succeed.

He extended his hand. "Meredith? Hi. Jace Moore."

Meredith accepted the handshake, noticing the roughness of his palm, then quickly let go. Who was she kidding? She very much wanted him to look her way. What woman wouldn't?

Only, he didn't.

She tamped down a tug of disappointment, and then guilt washed over her. Thoughts like that betrayed her friend. "Thanks for coming over. I'm looking to have an indoor riding arena built that is attached to the stable. I'd like it to be as big as I can afford. I have a folder here with a list of what I need, as well as rough sketches."

He gave her a smile that would knock the socks off of any self-respecting woman. "Let's take a look at the stable, then your notes."

"This way." Meredith firmed her resolve not to be charmed by this man. She knew his type. A man similar to her own father—a scoundrel when it came to women.

They walked down the sloping path from her driveway and the summer sun beat down on her back. She'd had time to change out of her work clothes into more comfortable jeans and a T-shirt, but a bead of sweat running down her temple made her wish she'd worn shorts regardless of how bad she looked in them.

"I saw your sign out front. What does RR Equine Therapy entail?"

Meredith slowed her pace to walk in step with him. She'd never expected to be this thrown off by the man, so she straightened her shoulders. "I work with emotionally at-risk kids, and getting them involved with horses often helps them work through issues. The bond they make with the horse can settle anxiety, help overcome past trauma and provide a host of other benefits including a new source of confidence."

Jace nodded. "Interesting."

"Horses are what got me through my teens," Meredith added and then mentally kicked herself. Why'd she say that? She didn't want to open that door, especially to someone like him.

"What does the *RR* stand for?"

Relief filled her. He hadn't picked up on her cryptic comment about growing up. "It stands for Rose River, but can also represent Rest and Renewal, or Respect and Redemption. At least, that's how I like to think of it."

Jace nodded, not looking at all like he understood the fluid interpretations of her business name. "So you've always had horses?"

"Not growing up. My neighbors did, and they gave me Bella as a graduation present but continued to board her until I had a place of my own. I bought Pete after college and the two have been with me ever since." Meredith opened the sliding barn door and was enveloped with cooler air. The stable was protected from the hot sun by the shade of mature maple trees.

"How long have you lived here? I seem to remember this used to be the Montgomery place."

Jace's dark eyes looked friendly enough, but there was no depth in them, no real caring.

Why Liza had ever gone out with a guy like him was a puzzle. Her friend was so grounded and kind. Surely, it hadn't just been about the man's looks.

Meredith came back to the conversation, knowing Jace didn't really care about her answer, but she'd give him all the facts he might need to know. "I bought the place five years ago." An inheritance from her paternal grandmother, who'd died when Meredith was twelve, had provided her downpayment. "I moved to Rose River to take a counseling job in the village of Hillman. My equine therapy program morphed out of bringing a client home who responded well to working with horses. I filed for a nonprofit and applied for a private grant that I landed. The grant is specifically for the arena, so that's all the money I have to work with. The goal is to continue sessions through the winter months without worries of ice and snow."

Meredith stood on the drain in the middle of the concrete floor, wondering how much of that he'd actually heard.

Jace looked around the stable containing four horse stalls and a tack room, but his gaze stopped on a painting of a horse she had hanging on the wall. The scripture from Matthew, Chapter 11, Verse 29, was etched onto the canvas and he read it aloud. "'Take my yoke upon you, and learn of me. For I am meek and lowly in heart, and ye shall find rest unto your souls.' So...is your therapy faith-based?"

Meredith nodded. "Yes. God works through the horses."

"And you, too." Jace actually gave her an admiring nod.

That surprised her. He knew about God, of course, from church, but his acceptance of her faith instead of cynicism was interesting considering what she'd heard about him from Liza. "I hope so. I'm not very preachy."

"The best kind of representation." Again, Jace looked around. "Speaking of which, where are the horses?"

"The pasture through that door." She pointed.

"Did you grow up in a Christian home?"

It was a casual enough question, but Meredith knew he was simply making small talk. "No." *Not even close.* "You?"

"Yeah." He peeked into a couple of stalls. "Wow, you keep it clean."

She'd put down interlocking rubber mats on the floor of each stall. "The mats are gentle on the horses' hooves and easy to hose down. Part of my program can be mucking stalls."

"Nice way to get the job done." He gave her a wink, as if he was in on her game.

Meredith felt her hackles rise, but she bit back a sharp response. Equine therapy wasn't a game.

Bonding with her horse had saved her from who knew what when her parents divorced, but she didn't need to prove anything to Jace Moore. She simply needed to land Three Sons Construction's services to build her arena and then be done with him and his lady-killer looks.

"All part of the program." She forced a smile.

He walked to the other end of the stable and the sliding barn door there. "Can I open this?"

"The horses might try to come in. Are you okay with that?"

"Of course." He didn't look as confident as his words.

And that made Meredith chuckle. "Let me close the one behind us first."

After she'd done that, he slid the door open, and sure enough, her mare, Bella, trotted toward them.

Jace backed up, looking nervous. "Coming in a little fast."

Pleased that his cocky grin was gone, Meredith attempted to allay his fears. At least a little. "Don't worry, she won't run you over. She's just curious."

Bella stopped at the door, shook her head and snorted.

Meredith opened a stall door for Bella, and soon her other horse, Pete, entered the building, too, their hooves clip-clopping on the cement until they entered their respective stalls.

Meredith closed the doors and turned to Jace.

"The dark one is Bella, and this big, blond fellow is Pete."

"They're both big." Jace stepped toward Bella. "Will she bite?"

"No. She hasn't ever. She wants to be petted." Meredith didn't bother to keep the challenge out of her voice.

Jace must have picked up on that. His gaze narrowed and then he cautiously reached out his hand and touched Bella's nose.

The mare drew closer and brushed his arm with her muzzle. Up and down.

Jace smiled as he lightly stroked the horse's neck. "She's a beauty."

"Yes." The horse had given Meredith's soul rest. She still did.

She waited for Jace to move away from Bella, so he could assess the best location for the arena, but the guy stayed put as if entranced with petting her horse. And then Bella did what she did best. As if sensing a need, the horse tipped her head to look Jace in the eyes and the two made some sort of connection. Moved by the gentle way Jace then leaned his forehead onto Bella's, Meredith held her breath.

As he gave her one more scratch behind her ears, Jace barely whispered, "She's an incredibly beautiful animal."

"I know." Meredith kept her voice soft and

quiet, too, wondering if she'd imagined what she'd witnessed.

Then he straightened, as if remembering why he'd come. "Okay, then. Let's see where the best place for the arena might be and then we can talk size."

Meredith walked through the open barn door toward the pasture. "There's a slope, but I don't want to lose stalls if I don't have to. Attaching the arena here, I'd lose pasture space, but I could expand the fencing eventually."

"You've only got two horses," Jace said.

"For now. This arena will help me grow. Right now, I have only three clients." She couldn't fail now. Not with an indoor arena.

Ever since Meredith had interned at an equine therapy farm downstate, she dreamed of building her own program. She hoped to do equine therapy full-time, maybe eventually bring on a few volunteers and another therapist. Maybe one with an occupational background so they could serve physical needs in addition to emotional ones.

But that was down the road. Way down the road. *If* she could raise the funds. *If* her program became better known in Rose River and *if* Jace Moore's company agreed to take on her project.

Jace made some scribbles, and a few quick calculations based on Meredith Lewis's notes. This job was definitely bigger than anticipated, but worth it. Rose River lay in the middle of a semi-agricultural area, so a job well done here could mean good word of mouth that might lead to more jobs like this, more barn structures in the community.

He turned toward Meredith. "I'll need to run some numbers and get back to you."

"Understood." Meredith nodded.

Standing nearly as tall as his six-foot frame, he looked her in the eyes easily enough. She must be close to his age, and had the prettiest blue eyes, fringed with thick lashes that looked golden. Her skin was smooth, but covered with freckles. He wouldn't call her pretty in the conventional sense, but she had a natural freshness about her that he found appealing. Her flaming red hair made him think of those Irish step dancers. He wondered if Meredith Lewis danced.

Not that he'd ask her out. She was a possible client and he wasn't dating casually anymore. Wasn't interested in dating, period. He needed to focus on getting his head together and face the gaping hole he had inside.

Jace looked around the vast property. She did have a neighbor across the street. Not too far away, but otherwise she was isolated out here. "Do you live here alone?"

She looked surprised by his question. "Umm, yes. Why?"

Her clients were kids, but a decent-size teenage boy could overpower her. She might be tall, but she was reed-thin and sort of delicate-looking, like what he'd imagine Shakespeare had in mind for Ophelia. Jace had studied the playwright in high school as an elective and had actually enjoyed it.

"These at-risk kids, do any have a history of violence?" Jace shuddered to think of someone raising a hand to that beautiful, dark horse, much less her owner.

Meredith looked perfectly at ease. "I meet with these kids in group settings at the center first and usually one-on-one before introducing them here. But in the future, with an indoor arena, I could expand to handle group sessions with kids in the legal system."

Jace nodded, unsure what that meant. He shouldn't care about whom she brought home, but something about Meredith made him feel a little protective. Maybe it was the odd connection he'd felt with her horse rather than the woman her-self—that had to be it. For a moment, it was as if Bella could see straight into his soul and read the pain there. It still hurt to think about his parents, who'd been killed in a snowmobile accident when he was fourteen. He'd thought about them every day since.

Jace climbed out of that mental rabbit hole and focused on Meredith. "Give me a couple of days and I'll be in touch."

"Thank you."

"Can I keep your notes and take a few pictures?"

"Of course. Go where you need to. I've got horses to feed now that they're inside."

"I won't be long." Jace slapped his folio shut with a snap and headed for his truck to toss the binder inside.

As he watched her walk back into the stable, Jace wondered what her therapy sessions might be like. Maybe he'd check it out one day if he got the job. He walked the property, taking pictures of the stable, the pasture and even the small outdoor arena, along with everything in between, before he left.

Once behind the wheel, he glanced around Meredith's place one more time. She had an older, white farmhouse that was neither large nor small. The stable looked newer than the house, and it had been built well, with white pine board-and-batten siding. He'd like to make the arena match somehow. Maybe tie it in with similar wood barn doors. She had twenty-five acres all told, according to the plat map he'd looked up before he came, so there was plenty of room for equipment and crew.

Jace started the engine, then glanced at the clock. It was after seven. He'd been here a long time—the longest he'd ever spent on an inspection for an estimate. But this was a different sort of project. Though he was drawn toward the cause and that beautiful horse, it was Meredith Lewis who intrigued him. Just how good was this program she ran, and did it really help?

* * *

Jace pulled into the driveway of the house he'd lived in his whole life. This was where his father had started the construction business that he and his two brothers ran. It's where his oldest brother, John, had raised him and Jeremy after their parents had died. Even after all these years, Jace still expected to see his mom on the front porch watering her many hanging plants and flowers.

Shaking off the bittersweet memory that kicked him in the gut, Jace shut off the engine and headed inside. He stepped into the kitchen and inhaled a delicious aroma. They all pitched in to make dinners, but tonight he was glad it wasn't his turn to cook. "What's for dinner?"

Jeremy turned from the stove, where he was swirling something in a huge, cast-iron pan. "Chicken stir-fry. You're fortunate I was late getting it started."

"Smells good. Hi, Mizz Mol." Jace bent down to pet Molly, Jeremy's Jack Russell-Lab mix. She'd walked toward him with her whole back end wiggling and a well-worn stuffed toy in her mouth.

"How'd it go?" John had entered the kitchen from the family room, where the TV was tuned to a local news station.

Jace opened the fridge and grabbed a can of pop. He set his zippered folio down on the table and cracked open the tab. "She wants to attach the indoor arena to the current stable. I have some pictures and notes we can go over later." He took a long drink, knowing he'd need John's input on this one.

"Sounds good."

"Where is it?" Jeremy asked.

"On County Line Road about six miles out of town. The old Montgomery place." Jace took another drink. "It's a solid project. She has the money in the form of a grant specifically for this, but—"

"But what?" John asked.

"Her business is a nonprofit. If funds are tight, maybe we can do a break on the labor." Jace wasn't sure why he'd said that. Why he'd even think it.

"Why's that?" John's eyes narrowed.

Jeremy snickered.

Jace ignored his younger brother. "It's a good cause."

Jeremy laughed out loud. "Cause? What cause? You don't get behind causes."

Jace felt his defenses kick in. "She works with at-risk kids. It's equine therapy."

"At risk for what?"

"I don't know. Emotion stuff." Jace realized that Meredith hadn't really clarified.

John's eyebrows rose.

Jeremy turned off the burner and brought the covered pan to the table. "Is this woman married?"

"What's that got to do with anything?" Jace asked.

"It's got everything to do with a discount." His little brother wiggled his eyebrows.

"Trust me, she's not my type. It's the program I think we should get behind." Jace didn't dare mention that he wanted to do right by a horse named Bella or he'd never hear the end of it.

"The entire female population is your type," Jeremy continued.

"At least I go out with women, instead of being scared of them," Jace teased back.

That only made Jeremy laugh more, his cover for everything. "Look who's calling the kettle black."

"Can we pray?" John interjected. "I'm hungry."

"Sure. Fine." Jace grabbed the pan of rice from the stove and set it on the table.

His younger brother was right. The last woman he'd dated had certainly scared him when she started talking about a future together. And *that* had been the end of her. Jace had slipped back into his old ways for a bit, but had stopped. He knew it wasn't right. He hadn't gone out with anyone since. If he didn't get his issues worked out, he'd end up alone. Maybe for good.

The three of them sat down and John did the honors of saying grace and then it was a free-for-all. They fell silent as they worked on clearing their plates, but then Jace finally asked his older brother, "What happened with the cutbacks on that reno? Is the client okay with them?"

John finished chewing, then swallowed half his glass of water before answering. "They accepted them. We're not doing the coffered ceiling, so that saved them some money."

Jace bowed out of contract disputes, leaving John to handle it. Jace didn't do confrontation if he didn't have to. He didn't do messiness. Of any sort.

Still, a lot of interior design work had been chopped, so Jace asked, "How'd Leah take the changes?"

"She rolled with it. I've got another renovation estimate tomorrow morning, but then I can swing by your arena and take a look."

"Meredith will most likely be at her job in Hillman." Jace was grateful for John's oversight.

Hiring Leah as part of their team had helped them grow into higher-end projects and more additions. It seemed like everybody watched those renovation TV shows and wanted a designer. Leah did her own thing as well, but most of her work came through them. Her services wouldn't be needed for a riding arena. He'd take direction from Meredith directly on the interior.

"Now, about this arena." John pushed away his empty plate. "Let's see what notes you have."

After he and Jeremy looked everything over, John said, "Do you mind making up a rough plan tonight? After I check the site, I'll drop it off to the engineer and look at pulling permits. Let's see where we come in before doing any discounts. You said the money's coming from a grant?"

"Yep. That's all in the notes." Jace loaded his plate in the dishwasher. "I'll draw up preliminary plans. I've got nothing going on tonight."

"What? No dates?" Mischief twinkled in his little brother's eyes.

"Not on a weeknight." Jace was done with dating. At least for now. Casual wasn't working anymore. It no longer distracted him from that void inside. Even after coming back to church, the empty abyss lay there, waiting to pounce.

He'd stopped being mad at God long ago, but had kept his distance until recently. Now, Jace wanted to focus on his spiritual health. He needed internal peace and figured it was time to let God grant him some, even though his fear of connecting with others remained strong.

He'd gotten counseling from the pastor about it but he'd suggested that Jace might need professional help. That wasn't something Jace was comfortable with. He didn't even know where to begin. He'd looked up a few therapists online, but didn't delve any further. He didn't want to seek out a psychiatrist, either. Going into a medical office seemed so sterile and intimidating. He needed—

"Did she say she was looking at other builders?" John brought the conversation back to the arena.

"I think we're her last hope. She'd received a high estimate from a company downstate and another wouldn't come out to inspect, and another only dealt in traditional pole barns."

John nodded. "Looks like we're it."

"It'll be a good project." Jace wanted to do it. "Good exposure for us."

"I hope you're right," John said.

"I am." Jace hoped so, too.

This might be different than most of their jobs, but it could open up new avenues of business for them. Not to mention that Jace was curious to find out what Meredith's equine therapy was all about. Maybe, just maybe, her sessions might be a right fit for him.

Chapter Two

Meredith checked the clock on her desk at work and decided to knock off early at half past three. Jace Moore and his crew were starting construction today and she wanted to see what they'd done. She also wanted to get accustomed to Jace's presence. The other two brothers of Three Sons Construction were evidently needed elsewhere, so Jace was in charge of her project. That meant she'd have to deal with him directly.

It had been three long weeks since Jace had first stopped by to put together an estimate. Since then, they'd talked on the phone a couple of times and Jace had come to the house to go over plans and tweaked costs. In spite of her reservations about the man, she appreciated that he'd stayed within her grant budget.

Every conversation had been centered on the riding arena, as it should. He'd been brief, professional and friendly, but that last in-person visit to the house, when they'd walked to the stable, Jace hadn't gone near Bella. It made her wonder if whatever connection she thought she'd seen between horse and man had been her imagination.

Now, Meredith pulled into her driveway and smiled. Two pickup trucks parked in a line. They'd kindly left an open spot for her. Seeing the newer, navy truck bearing the Three Sons Construction logo made her heart skip a beat, but Meredith dismissed the reaction as excitement for her arena finally coming to fruition. It had nothing to do with the man who drove that truck.

Yeah, right.

Ignoring her own mocking thoughts, she shut off the engine. She glanced toward the horse stable and spotted a bulldozer. Jace and his crew were making the ground ready and it looked like they'd gotten a lot done if the huge flat area of dirt was any indication.

Meredith shouldered her purse and hopped out of her pickup. As she walked toward the site, she took in the cleared ground, relieved that she'd agreed to attach the arena through a breezeway from the stable. With that flat space, she could visualize the building now, and knew it would look nice. Better than off the back.

She stopped by the side of dug-up dirt as Jace approached her. She had to shield her eyes from the sun, until his tall frame cast a shadow over her.

"What do you think?" he asked.

"I think this location is better." It was hard not to notice how great her builder looked in a pair of jeans and a Three Sons Construction T-shirt, his usual uniform.

"We should finish this up today, then tomorrow the base, along with drainage. After that, we'll build the structure before laying the final footing and top layer of sand."

Meredith nodded, but a new sense of tension coiled through her. This was finally happening and didn't get any more real. And scary. Could she make this business grow? Or was it all a pipe dream, as her mother had once said long ago?

She glanced at Jace. "Anything I can help with?"

"Nope, but thanks."

"Do you guys need water?"

"We're good." Jace grinned.

Be still my heart.

"Okay then, carry on." Meredith ignored that stellar smile of his and returned to her house.

She climbed the steps of her back porch and entered into the kitchen then leaned against the sink. She ignored the annoying sound of a dripping faucet and stared out the window at the building site beyond. Another good reason to build the arena on the west side of the stable, as Jace had suggested, was the view she had from her kitchen window. Watching a little while longer, hearing the *beep-beep-beep* of the bulldozer as it backed up, she thanked the Lord again for making this possible. Even if it meant enduring the nerve-wracking presence of Jace Moore.

Meredith darted upstairs to change out of her cotton pants and dressy T-shirt. She had notes to review regarding her young client's first equine therapy session this evening. She glanced at her watch and saw she had another hour or so before she had to feed the horses. Would the crew stop at five o'clock or did they work longer? She'd find out soon enough.

After slipping into a comfortable pair of jeans and an old T-shirt, she went back downstairs and powered up her laptop. She read through email, then moved onto her notes and made a plan for tonight's session. After a bit, Meredith heard a truck engine start in the driveway. Checking her watch, she saw that it was past five.

After saving her work, she got up from the dining room table and headed outside. Jace Moore's truck was still parked in her driveway. She spotted him by the bulldozer and walked over. "Done for the day?"

"Hey." He looked up from the tablet he held with what looked like blueprints on the screen. *Her blueprints.* "We're done. I'm just going over the plans for tomorrow."

Excitement percolated within her at the progress of a simple level spot. "Great. Well, I better feed the horses."

"Want some help?"

Meredith narrowed her gaze. "Do you really want to?"

"Actually, I do. I have some questions—" Jace smiled and lifted his tablet. "Let me put this away first."

"I'll get the horses and meet you inside the stable. They might be a little skittish with that bulldozer sitting there."

Jace nodded and jogged toward his truck.

Meredith slipped under the fence of the upper pasture. Why on earth did Jace Moore want to help her? He'd mentioned questions. Probably something about her notes.

She opened the stable door and whistled. It didn't take long for the horses to come. Pete trotted toward her without even a glance at the machinery. But Bella stopped when she spotted that big yellow bulldozer and eyed it as if the thing might jump over the fence.

"It's okay, girl," Meredith cooed.

The mare dropped her head, sniffed at the ground and contemplated her next move, but then she caught up with Pete and followed him into the stable.

"Bella, you're a silly girl." Meredith chuckled. She relished the familiar sweet smells of hay and horse as she opened the stall door.

Jace stepped in from the front entrance. "Okay to come in?"

"Of course."

He hesitated until the horses were secure in

their stalls, then walked toward her. "Thanks for letting me help. What do you feed them?"

"They get some fresh hay and I follow up with a little mix of grains and oats. Of course, they love treats like carrots and apples. They graze the pasture, but I still feed them daily to make sure they get enough of what they need."

He'd already tuned her out as he stepped up to Bella and petted her nose, then murmured, "Hello there, beauty."

Bella rubbed her face against his shoulder.

So that's why he wanted to help. Meredith smiled as she watched them get reacquainted. "She loves compliments."

"Don't we all?" Jace continued to scratch behind her mare's ears, his fingers threading through her dark mane.

"I don't know about that."

He spoke like a real Casanova. Or at least someone who knew how to work people. Meredith didn't really trust flattering remarks, not that she received many. Oh, her coworkers praised her efforts with clients and some of the women liked her casual outfits, but when had a guy given her a compliment? One she could actually believe?

Meredith was too tall and skinny with a mop of red hair. And she'd been teased her whole life about the freckles that covered her face and body. Really, who was going to be impressed by all that?

Jace glanced her way. "What's the matter, don't you like compliments?"

Meredith snorted. "Depends on the sincerity behind it."

He shrugged, looking like he wasn't interested in pursuing the battle. "I suppose you're right."

Meredith knew better than to trust the things men said. She'd had a boyfriend in college with a honeyed tongue who'd turned out to be unfaithful. The same went for her father. She'd never forgive, much less forget, the reason he'd left her mother. All because of her. If Meredith hadn't spoken up, would her parents have stayed together? Maybe. Maybe not.

She walked over to a corner of the stable where she kept square bales of hay. She pulled one down a little rougher than necessary and ended up tripping backward and landing on her backside.

"Whoa, I could have done that." Jace stepped forward.

Meredith waved him away. "I do this daily."

She didn't open a new bale every day, but she didn't need his help, either. Didn't need a man, period. At least that's what she'd told herself most of her adult life because she didn't want the inevitable heartache that came with dating. At twenty-eight, that philosophy had served her well. So why did she *want* this particular man, who had "bad for you" written all over him, to look her way and take notice?

She pulled the hay bale apart with gusto and handed a chunk to Jace. "Would you like to give this to Bella?"

He took the hay from her hands. "Just throw it in, or what?"

"You can hold it for her, or go into her stall and place it in the hay rack above her grain bowl." Meredith walked into Pete's stall and stuffed the fresh hay into the wire-basket feeder attached to the wall. "Like so."

He looked hesitant, but finally went in cautiously.

Bella snatched a bit of hay from his hands since Jace was too slow in getting it into the feeder. It was rather cute the way he gave up and hand-fed Bella. Jace remained watchful as he leaned against the wall of the stall, still holding hay out with his palms up. Bella took her time, being careful, too.

And Meredith hadn't imagined it. There was definitely a sweet connection between the two.

Jace wasn't too sure about being in a confined space with such a large animal, but he didn't get trampled and the delicate way Bella gobbled up the hay from his hands made him relax. A little. "Is this what you do in equine therapy?"

Meredith had come out of Pete's stall, and now rested her arms on the edge of Bella's stall and looked in at him. "Yes and no. I try to tailor the sessions to the individual and give them tasks with the horse to open a connection. Horses can sense our feelings. Bella knows you're nervous, so she's trying to be careful around you. Just relax."

He breathed in, then exhaled. "Is it that obvious?"

"Just to me. Never been around horses?"

"Nope. Never." Although, he could get used to this. There was something calming about stroking the horse's silky smooth skin. Something peaceful. "We have a dog and cats at home."

"We?" Meredith looked curious, but not in an are-you-single kind of way.

Jace knew that look all too well and Meredith just didn't have it. In fact, she was direct and professional. He liked that. They'd met now on a couple of occasions and Meredith Lewis didn't appear to have a flirtatious bone in her body. If anything, she was standoffish with him. Not that he minded. He wasn't checking her out. She was *his* client for one, and Jace didn't get involved with clients. Secondly, he might want to take her equine therapy, which would make him a patient of hers and, no doubt, doubly off-limits.

He realized that he hadn't answered her question. As he continued handing hay to Bella, who liked taking it from his hands better than from the wire feeder on the wall, Jace said, "My brothers and me."

"As in Three Sons Construction."

He nodded. "John, me and Jeremy. We share

the house we grew up in. Jeremy has a habit of bringing home strays. The dog and cats are his."

"Nice." She didn't say more, but waited for him to elaborate.

He didn't.

Another thing he'd noticed about Meredith Lewis was that she listened intently. She looked at him with those pretty blue eyes of hers and simply waited. She didn't rush ahead or try to answer for him. He kind of liked that, too.

He looked away. "Yeah, it works."

Jace could have explained that there hadn't been any reason for them to move out. John had had a few girlfriends in the past, but they never stuck around. No doubt, they didn't appreciate competing for John's attention between his brothers and the business.

Although lately, Jace wondered if John might have a *thing* for their interior designer. Not that he'd bring that subject up anytime soon. John would shut down that conversation quickly. Neither he nor Jeremy had serious relationships. Ever since the breakup with his high-school sweetheart, Jeremy didn't even date. He went out with a mixed group of friends.

Jace glanced at Meredith, with her flaming hair pulled back into its usual thick braid. Some of it curled around her face, making him wonder what all that hair might look like loose. "What about you? Any brothers or sisters?"

A curtain seemed to close over those sky-blue eyes. "Nope. Just me."

"Only child." He hated to think what might have happened to him had he been all alone after his folks died, if it hadn't been for John keeping the three of them together.

"Yup." She glanced at her watch and grimaced. "Look, I've got a first-timer coming for equine therapy—"

"Sure. Sorry, I'll get going then." Jace straightened and brushed hay from his hands. He exited Bella's stall.

"It's not right away, but I have to eat something." Meredith opened the front barn-door entrance and let him walk through first, leaving it open behind her. "I'm just making a sandwich but you're more than welcome to one, too."

Jace chuckled as he walked beside her toward the house and his truck. It was a tempting offer. Not so much for the food, but the company. He liked talking to Meredith.

"Thank you, but no. I should get home. In fact, I think it's my night to cook."

"What are you making?" A slight smile curved her plump lips.

It struck him that she had a very kissable mouth. Jace shrugged off *that* thought. "Probably calling in a couple pizzas."

"Pizza is always good." She walked him to his truck.

"It is." He kicked at the ground, curious about her upcoming session. "Is this patient an adult?"

Meredith tipped her head. "Tonight? No. And I have *clients*, not patients. I'm no doctor. This is the boy's first session and more of an introduction to the horses. His mom will be with him as well."

"How old is he?"

Meredith wrinkled her nose. It made her look cute. "Twelve."

Jace wished he could see how this equine therapy worked before he asked specifics about the services she offered. "Would I be able to observe a session?"

"You want to watch?"

He didn't want to put himself out there if it wasn't something that might help him. Thinking quick, he offered, "I'd like to see how the arena will be used and if the observation booth we planned is in the right spot. If it's allowed."

Meredith looked thoughtful. "Not usually, no, due to confidentiality. Right now, parents only attend for the first session. Kids don't really open up if their folks can hear them. That's why that booth is important. It'll get them out of sight and earshot."

"The parents," Jace reiterated.

"Yes. And eventually group home supervisors. Offering group sessions will be an option year-round with kids out of the elements in winter. Anyway, all I have now are a few equine therapy clients from Hillman. The kid tonight, and then two on Thursday nights."

No wonder the arena was a big deal. "Makes sense. Well, I'll let you go. See you tomorrow, Meredith."

"Yup. See you tomorrow."

He climbed into his truck, and called in a pizza order for pick-up. He'd make a quick salad at home and call it good. Backing out of the driveway, he noticed a mostly white cat with dark markings on its face in one of the windows of Meredith's house. It dawned on him that he hadn't seen any cats in the stable. He thought all barns had cats.

But then he thought all women liked compliments and Meredith didn't appear to care for them. She was definitely different from the women he used to hang around—women who didn't make him think too much, or demand much more than a good time. Except for Liza—she'd been too good for him.

Now, he wanted more than a good time, but couldn't quite cross that bridge. He couldn't open up and be real with anyone other than his brothers. And even with them, he tended to be the don't-make-waves kind of guy he'd been for so long. Could Meredith's equine therapy help him bridge the gap between who he really was and who he presented himself to be? Somehow, he'd have to find out.

Chapter Three

The following day when Meredith came home, she spotted a big dump truck near the bulldozer. She exited her pickup and ran over to the leveled ground that had been filled in with crushed stone. She approached Jace, who was looking over the area, his tablet in hand once again.

"This looks good."

Jace turned and smiled at her. "We contracted out to a company downstate that specializes in riding-arena foundations. That's their dump truck."

Meredith smiled back. "This is moving right along."

"The building will take some time, but we'll get it done. How'd your session go with the young boy?"

"It went well. The kid was scared and put on a tough front, but Pete waited quietly by his side. When Tommy finally reached out and petted Pete, his mom was nearly in tears. Thank you for asking." Flattered that he'd not only remembered, but also looked like he really wanted to know,

Meredith was glad she'd asked Tommy's mom if her builder could observe a session. His interest showed that he really cared about this structure.

"Were you in the stable?" Jace asked.

"The outdoor arena. We only have so many nice summer evenings left."

"Yeah, don't remind me." Jace's brow furrowed.

Meredith chuckled. "Don't you like winter?"

"Not much." Jace shrugged.

"You live in the wrong state."

"So I've been told. An indoor arena will make a big difference in your work," Jace added, as if finally seeing that for himself.

"Huge. Year-round sessions without weather worries." She couldn't keep from spilling out her dreams, her excitement. "I hope to grow enough to need volunteers and also bring on another therapist and more horses to meet needs."

Last night, Meredith had held her breath while young Tommy stood in front of Pete. But the horse seemed to know how broken Tommy's spirit had been. Broken because the kid's father had left them—something she could relate to.

"It's a good thing you do here. I'm interested in… Maybe…" Jace looked away. "Volunteering."

The heightened color around his ears surprised her. What was he saying? Or more likely, what was he not saying? And then an idea hit her. "Would you like to ride a horse?"

He took a step back. "Ah—"

"I mean, if you have time." Meredith glanced at Jace's footwear, glad to see his work boots had a heel.

"You're serious."

"Absolutely serious. The more at ease you are around my horses, the better you'll be at *volunteering*. Plus, both horses could really use a ride."

"Riding, huh?" He thought about it for a moment, then shrugged. "Sure, why not? Let me put my tablet away."

Meredith gathered up her liability forms from the file cabinet in the tack room while Jace stashed his electronic device in his truck. She hoped she didn't regret this, but she had to go for a trail ride, anyway, and having a second rider along would be nice for a change.

Plus, it wouldn't hurt to test Jace's mettle. Something was definitely up with him; he seemed overly curious about her sessions and maybe a ride would help her figure out why. If he was serious about volunteering, she didn't want to worry about how he handled the horses. The more experience he had, the more comfortable he'd be, and nothing gave a person more experience than riding.

Her therapy sessions didn't involve much riding at this point; it was more about getting the person to open up to the horse and connect. But her first client had eventually learned to ride. Jace already had a friendly connection with Bella. Now, he needed experience with her. Besides, keeping her horses healthy as well as happy was important and trail rides did both.

"Before we go, do you mind signing a waiver? If you change your mind after reading it, I'll totally understand."

Jace reached for the forms. "No problem, but just for the record, I wouldn't sue you if I fell off."

Meredith couldn't risk it. Her liability insurance was high enough as it was. "I think I'll have you ride Bella. Pete naturally takes the lead and Bella is less likely to spook when she follows."

"Spook?" Jace looked nervous.

"Horses are prey animals, so their response to perceived danger is to flee."

"What danger?" Jace looked like he might be the one to flee as he handed back the signed forms.

Meredith chuckled. "Oh, little things like a plastic bag blowing across the path."

"Maybe I should pass. If I do fall off, I can't afford to get hurt and delay your arena."

"I didn't mean to scare you, but I want you to be prepared just in case. In the saddle, you have to stay alert, ready to react. Plus, we'll wear helmets. I'll show you what to do and we won't go far." Meredith looked at him, then opened the sliding barn door to the pasture and threw down a challenge. "Are you in?"

"I'm in." His eyes had darkened, or maybe it was just the lack of bright light.

She whistled, and Pete and Bella trotted in. Meredith secured a lead rope to each horse's halter, which she then tied to different hooks on the wall.

She motioned for Jace to follow her, and then slipped the forms back into the file cabinet. She'd take them inside later. "The saddles and bridles are in the tack room. I'll have you watch me with Pete, then I'll walk you through the same process with Bella."

"Sounds good." Jace looked really serious.

"Relax, this will be fun—I promise."

"If you say so." Anticipation shone from his dark eyes. He seemed less nervous and more excited, which was a good thing.

Meredith didn't force anyone to overcome their fears. When it came to her work, it was a gradual process that she moved along by encouraging her clients to face their fears. This might not be a session, but seeing Jace conquer his nerves about riding seemed important. As much to him as it was to her.

Inside the tack room, Jace chose a helmet that fit him, but he fumbled with the strap. "Can you tighten it?"

She stepped forward and threaded the strap for him to pull tight. "Got it?"

He looked at her. "Yeah, thanks."

Standing this close, Meredith realized Jace's eyes were actually a muddy gray, not brown. She really shouldn't contemplate how nice they were, or how easy it might be to get lost in them.

Nope, not going there. This man is a heart-breaker.

She stepped away, quickly gathered up the saddle pad and headed into the main stable. She placed the blanket on Pete's back, then returned to the tack room for the saddle and bridle, giving step-by-step instructions on how to place each on the horse.

Pete did his usual little sidestep as she tightened up the strap around his belly. "We'll tighten the cinch again before we get on."

"He doesn't look too happy about that saddle."

Meredith waved away his concern. "He's just getting comfortable."

She walked Jace through saddling up Bella and checked his work. All good. She coached him through putting the bridle on and was pleased to hear him whisper into Bella's ear to go easy on him since he was a newbie.

Bella responded with a nose rub against his shoulder.

Meredith adjusted the stirrups for Jace's height and tightened the cinch. Now, they were ready to climb aboard, so Meredith showed Jace how to mount up. It took a couple of attempts, but then he swung his leg over and sat in the saddle perfectly, as if it came naturally. She mounted up and went over a quick lesson in reining and when to apply pressure with his legs.

"We'll get used to walking around the pasture first, 'til you feel comfortable," she continued as she donned her own helmet.

Jace nodded, concentrating on keeping his balance.

"Just relax, and keep your heels down and in line with your hips and shoulders. Try standing in the stirrups using the balls of your feet. That's the only contact you want on the flat part of the stirrup. Do not point your toes down or let your foot fall through, for obvious tangle reasons. See?" Meredith stood to show Jace.

He did the same.

"Feel balanced?"

"I do."

"Good. Give Bella a pat, especially when she obeys your reining. Pressing your legs to her sides will tell her to move forward, or go faster, so you don't want to hang on with your legs. You'll want to move with her motion using the balls of your feet, like so." Meredith demonstrated. "It's called posting. But you'll see."

They took a few turns around the pasture, walking the horses down and back so Jace could get the hang of neck reining. He seemed more relaxed and comfortable in the saddle, so she asked, "Ready to go on the trail?"

He took a big breath and let it out. "I think so."

"Alright then, let's do this." Meredith dismounted to open the gate, then mounted back up and led the way toward the multipurpose trail system.

She glanced at Jace, who gave her a crooked smile. She could tell he was enjoying this and that was a positive sign for things to come—working with the horses. The only negative was how good he looked in the saddle. Meredith didn't need any more reasons to find Jace Moore attractive.

Jace followed Meredith, or rather Bella followed Pete. He grew accustomed to the swaying motion of the horse's walk and relaxed. Leaning forward a little, he scratched between her ears. "You're a sweet horse."

Bella nodded as if she understood.

Jace wondered how many words horses could understand. Jeremy had told him many times that dogs comprehended up to fifty. Were horses smarter than dogs? More perceptive maybe, since entire therapy practices had been built around them.

He watched Meredith in front of him. She looked good on a horse, like she belonged out here amid the trees, where the sunshine dappled through the leaves. She was as natural as the faded jeans and ratty Superman T-shirt she was wearing.

Once again, he compared Meredith to the women he'd gone out with. How many of those ladies would ever wear an old T-shirt, as if appearance didn't matter?

"How are you doing back there?" Meredith asked.

"Good," he answered honestly. There was something freeing about being on a horse. He felt connected with the earth below and the sky above, and even the trees surrounding them. The muffled sound of Bella's hooves hitting the soft ground was oddly soothing. This sense of freedom must be what drew men to become cowboys.

When the path widened, Meredith slowed Pete and moved right so that Bella could walk up beside them. "It stays wide like this for a while. Plus, I want to see how you're holding the reins. Good. Nice and relaxed."

"Thanks for inviting me to do this." Jace meant it. In fact, he'd like to do it again.

"Thanks for going through with it. I either take turns riding them alone or hook one up to the other so they both go. They like riding together, though. Horses are social animals. They don't do well alone."

"Neither do we." Even with the walls and roadblocks he'd put up, Jace liked being around people. He'd always been an extrovert, but a surface-level one. He didn't go deep. He couldn't. Could equine therapy change that?

"True. So have you always worked construction?" she asked.

"I have."

"Never wanted to do anything else?"

"Nope." Obviously, she hadn't heard about his folks. Maybe it was old news after sixteen years, but it still felt fresh for him, especially near the holidays. There were days when memories would sneak up on him at the oddest moments and literally steal his breath away.

Jace glanced at Meredith. Maybe he should give her his backstory before asking to sign up for equine therapy. She was surprisingly easy to talk to, which spoke volumes for *her* career choice. A career choice he hoped could help him. "My father started the business. Back then it was called My Three Sons Construction. My brother John took over when my parents died. They were killed in a snowmobile accident right before Christmas when I was fourteen."

Her face softened, but she looked composed. No doubt, she'd heard worse. "I'm so sorry. That must have been very difficult."

It still is.

"John stepped in to raise me and Jeremy, keeping us together instead of shipping each of us off to our aunts downstate. He dropped out of college to devote his time to the business, and for that I'll always be grateful. As a teen, I helped John with odd jobs that I could do and more as he taught me. It didn't take long to realize that I didn't want to do anything else."

"How old was John when your parents died?" Meredith asked.

"Twenty."

"Wow. That's a lot of pressure on a young man."

Didn't he know it. Especially in the beginning. He and Jeremy fought a lot, but his little brother had fought against John's supervision even more. Jace remembered a time when Jeremy came at their older brother with fists flying. John took every blow and then held Jeremy until the fight went out of him. That's when Jace had decided to bury his own grief and anger in order to keep things smooth at home, for everyone's sake.

"Making our business grow is important to me, like payback for all that John did for us." Jace had never admitted that to anyone. Not even his brothers. It's what got him out of bed in the mornings.

"Does he expect payback?"

"Not at all. John encouraged us to attend college, try something else if we wanted to, but we didn't want to. I went to a building trade school, but Jeremy stayed home, content with working the business. He's a talented carpenter, mostly self-taught, and does our finish work."

Meredith gave him another soft smile, encouraging him. "You're tight with your brothers."

"We look out for each other, but it's still tough at Christmastime. My mom used to go all out with decorating and baking. We typically shut down the office and take trips around the holidays. Anything to get away from the memories, you know?"

Maybe he shouldn't have unloaded all that until she'd taken him on officially, but he knew his loss was part of why he couldn't settle down and commit. He couldn't even face Christmas.

"Yes. That makes sense." Meredith looked like she understood completely.

She also looked ready to counsel him, so he braced to hear what he'd heard before—that he needed to face those holidays and learn to accept what had happened.

He got trapped by the compassionate look in her blue eyes. Did she see why he didn't like the leaves changing—because that meant the holidays were near, along with the raw memories that came with them? But Meredith didn't speak. She simply waited for him to go on.

He chickened out and looked away. "Did you always want to be an equine therapist?"

"I didn't even know about it until I started looking at colleges and that sealed the deal. How'd you like to pick up the pace?"

"Pace?" A zip of enticement flew up his spine, but he knew better than to think she meant anything personal by it.

"The horses could use a little trot. Are you up for going faster?"

Jace swallowed hard. "Sure, let's do this."

"Okay, but first, remember what I said about

using the balls of your feet to lift up and move with the horse. That way you're not bouncing hard in the saddle. Keep your reins a little closer, but not tight. If you want to stop, rein back but then loosen up once Bella stops."

He gave her a cheeky grin. "Got it."

Meredith made a clicking sound, then said, "Giddy-up." Just like in the movies. Pete was ready to move and Bella followed, but it wasn't exactly fast. More like a bouncy jog.

Jace didn't want to slam his 190 pounds down on Bella, so he tried to move with her, coming up slightly from the saddle as Meredith demonstrated. At first it felt herky-jerky, but then suddenly, he was moving in sync with the horse. And it was great. In fact, he wanted to go faster.

Meredith slowed Pete when they came to a fork in the path. She reined left and Pete took the turn at a walk and headed for home. She turned in the saddle to make sure Jace did the same.

"Whoa, Bella girl." He wore an ear-to-ear grin as he reined Bella to not only follow, but also come up alongside her and Pete. He didn't look like a new rider at all. He looked rather competent.

"Nice job!" Meredith meant it.

"Did you expect anything less?" he quipped back with that charming smile of his.

Now, she knew his cocky front was just that. A cover for the pain he still carried inside. Fourteen was a tender age to lose his folks and it sounded as if he and his brothers hadn't fully dealt with or processed their grief if they still ran from the holidays.

Liza hadn't mentioned the Moore brothers' tragedy, but then it was long ago. Time wasn't always a healer. She knew that all too well. Her parents had split when she was only thirteen, and between her mother's bitterness and her father's indifference, it still messed with her head and heart. Her parents loved her on some level, they had to, but did they truly care?

But Jace had surprised her yet again. Not only had he agreed to a trail ride when he'd never been on a horse, but he'd also clearly enjoyed it. He had a sweetness that she liked behind the overly confident front. Fortunately, he didn't try to charm *her*. She had to own that she preferred the peer-like treatment from him, as if they were a team. He treated her with respect and she'd take that any day of the week.

"So when will we go faster than a trot?" Jace asked.

Meredith smiled. "Another time, after your muscles are used to this. You'll be sore tomorrow."

He gave her a no-way look.

"You'll see. We didn't go too far today because I didn't want to wreck your workday tomorrow."

"You're serious."

"I am." Meredith dismounted so she could close the pasture gate.

When they reached the stable, she walked Pete in, Bella following with the clop-clop of their hooves echoing through the space.

"Might as well put their halters on and hook them up while we take off their saddles and then give them a good brushing."

"Okay." Jace dismounted too.

Meredith hoisted off the saddle along with the pad beneath it. Inhaling the comforting smell of leather and light horse sweat, she said, "Come with me and we'll get brushes."

"Sure thing." Jace followed her into the tack room with Bella's saddle.

Meredith showed him where everything went, then offered him a curry comb from a basket filled with different brushes.

"What's that?" he asked.

"It's what I brush the horses with after a ride. Just slip your hand in under the strap, like so, and away you go." She lifted the basket. "There's other styles in here, too."

Jace took the curry comb.

They went back to the horses and Meredith showed Jace how to brush. "I usually start at their neck and work toward the hind end."

Jace was already gently brushing Bella's mane, whispering sweet nothings to her, and then he quieted as he focused on smoothing out the indentation marks left from the saddle's girth with both the comb and his other hand.

Meredith brushed Pete, patting the quarter horse, who was a gentle giant at seventeen hands—nearly sixty-eight inches tall.

"What kind of horse is she?" Jace finally asked.

"She's Arabian. That's why her face is more refined than Pete's. He's all quarter horse."

Jace ran his hand over Bella's back. He'd brushed her well, even taking care of her tail. "Now what?"

"Now, we give them a little grain reward and let them out to pasture." Meredith untied Pete's lead rope and walked him into his stall.

Jace did the same with Bella.

Meredith fetched a scoop of grain and deposited half in Pete's dish, then gave Jace the other half for Bella.

"Here you go, girl." He dumped the scoop into her grain bin but didn't leave. He stroked her neck while she ate.

Meredith folded her arms on Bella's stall and watched them.

Jace didn't fear standing close to the horses any longer. He was relaxed. Bella was, too. She stopped gobbling up her oats for a moment, turned and nuzzled Jace in the shoulder, leaving a trail of sloppy oat residue.

"Ugh. Nice." But Jace didn't look irritated. He looked smitten.

"She really likes you."

"I like her, too." Jace continued to caress her neck in long, therapeutic strokes.

Meredith knew her horses were gentle. They loved people and attention, and that made them great for equine therapy, but there was something different in the way Bella treated Jace. There was something encouraging in her mare's approach to the man. Bella seemed to be nudging Jace to open up and tell her his troubles. It reminded Meredith of the way Grandma Rose used to scoop her up into her lap for a snuggle when she was little, asking about her day and really wanting to know the answer.

She heard Pete shake his head. He wanted out. "I'm going to lead him out to the pasture, if you'd like to lead Bella."

"It looks like she's done eating."

Meredith opened the stall door. She didn't have to lead Pete, but she held on to his halter for Jace's sake. He was still a newbie, and Meredith didn't want Pete to cause a ruckus by rushing out the door.

Jace held on to the lower strap of Bella's harness and walked her out into the pasture. He let go but Bella didn't follow Pete's trot into the field. She stood next to Jace and waited.

"What does she want?" Jace asked.

"Not sure." Meredith shrugged, but suspected Bella knew there was unfinished business inside Jace. Feelings that needed to come out.

"You can go, girl. I'll be back." He ran his hand down her back and patted her rump.

The horse took off, trotting after Pete with her black tail held high and proud.

"Wow. She's really something," Jace said.

Meredith knew that in more ways than she could count. "Yup."

He turned his dark gray gaze on her. "No patients tonight?"

"No. And they're clients," Meredith said, correcting him again. "I'm no psychologist."

"That's right." Jace ran a hand through his hair. "But you're a counselor—licensed and all that?"

"I am, along with equine therapy certifications." Meredith tipped her head. "Why?"

"I respect what you do, so let me be upfront. I'm curious about more than just volunteering. Would your equine therapy be open to me?"

Meredith nearly dropped her curry comb. Suddenly his interest in observing her sessions made more sense. It wasn't about making sure the structure met her needs, it was about meeting his own. She hadn't expected this, but she shouldn't be surprised.

She tossed the comb in the basket. "I don't think that's a good idea."

"Why not?" Jace asked.

Meredith wasn't used to serving adults in equine therapy, much less an attractive man who happened to be her builder and the breaker of her friend's heart. But she couldn't deny there was something between Jace and Bella. Her mare had loosened the man's tongue out there on the trail, and obviously, he needed more.

"With you building my arena, there's a huge conflict of interest. I can refer you—"

He shook his head. "No. No way. I feel more comfortable talking with you, *because* I'm your builder."

Her heart sank and twisted. She was a sucker for someone who needed help. It's why she did what she did. But there were ethics to follow in her line of work—namely, do not befriend the clients. Had she already crossed that line? Probably.

"Maybe all I need is a couple of sessions. At least let me tell you why," Jace added.

She knew why. He hadn't properly dealt with his grief. She could at least hear him out. "Come on in the house and we'll talk."

Meredith needed to put away her preconceived opinions of Jace Moore and hope that the attraction she felt for him would be extinguished, too. Like snuffing out a candle, she needed that flame put out for good. Her license and her career might depend on it.

Chapter Four

Jace walked into Meredith's homey kitchen and looked around. He'd been in here once before to go over plans, but hadn't taken in the decor. His gaze roamed the white cupboards with black iron hardware and a butcher-block-topped island strategically placed under a cast-iron pot hanger that even their interior designer, Leah, would approve of.

The late summer breeze lifted lace curtains from an open window on the far wall. He noticed the same lace hanging in the open window over the sink. Healthy green plants littered the sill. He finally said, "You have a nice place here."

Meredith smiled. "Thanks. Can I offer you some lemonade?"

"Please." Jace bent to pet the cat that bumped its head against his leg. "Hey, kitty."

"That's Willem."

"Like the actor?"

"Doesn't he look like Willem Dafoe?"

Jace laughed and looked closer. "Now that you mention it, he does."

He slipped onto the stool tucked under the island's overhang and watched Meredith grab a glass and then fill it with ice. She moved with effortless grace. Something he hadn't noticed before—and shouldn't be noticing now. The sound of a faucet drip caught his attention, so he got up to check it out.

"That drip just started. Not sure why."

"Let's take a look." Jace ducked underneath the sink and saw that everything was dry, so he turned off the water supply. "I'll grab my tools and be right back."

"Oh, well, okay." Meredith set two glasses of lemonade on the island.

Jace left to grab his toolbox from the truck. He pulled his phone out of his back pocket and texted his brothers to go ahead and eat dinner without him. He wasn't sure when he'd be home.

He received an immediate ding from Jeremy. Who is she?

Arena client. Going over plans, Jace texted back. He wasn't completely truthful, but it wasn't exactly a lie, either.

His brothers didn't need to know he was seeking professional help from Meredith. But Meredith had said he was a conflict of interest. Would she take him on? He hoped so. He felt way more comfortable talking to her out here than going into some sterile doctor's office.

Jeremy sent him a winking emoji while John simply replied with a plain, old okay.

Jace headed back into Meredith's kitchen and went straight for the faucet. He unscrewed the hot-water side handle and found that the nut was pretty loose. He tightened it up, turned the water back on and tested it.

"You're all set," he said as he closed up his toolbox.

"That was quick. How'd you know it was the hot-water side?"

Jace shrugged and reached for the lemonade. "Just a hunch." He took a drink. "This is good."

Meredith lifted the icy pitcher with lemons floating around. "More?"

Jace held out his glass. "Absolutely."

"I'm not agreeing to take you on as a client, but here is a questionnaire I give out before the start of sessions in order to clarify your goals." Meredith handed him a few sheets of paper.

He sat back down and glanced over them. The first page explained the sessions in a general way and listed the hourly fee. He could swing that, no problem. The second page covered typical medical history and emergency contact stuff, but the third had mental-health history questions and a list of disorders with a check box next to them.

He looked up at her. "I don't think these apply to me."

"Try the last page."

The last page had only a few questions about methods of coping with uncomfortable feelings and then a checkoff list of horse experience and interests.

Again, he looked at Meredith. "Can I be honest?"

Meredith nodded. "Of course."

"I have trouble connecting with people, other than on a surface level. That's what I want to fix."

Meredith looked wary, as if she didn't quite take him at his word. But then, she was in social work, so she probably heard a lot of blown smoke. He'd heard that some in that field followed the people-are-basically-good mantra. He knew better than to believe that philosophy. As the pastor of his church was known to say, God wouldn't have needed to send his Son to die for the sins of the world if that world was inherently good.

Jace wasn't good regardless of what Meredith believed. She was hard to read, except when she was around her horses. The joy in her face had been easy enough to see when she'd taught him to ride.

"It's possible to get to the root cause through interaction with Bella," she said slowly.

"I know my parents' death is the root cause. I just don't know how to change it. How to change *me*." Old habits were hard to break and he had plenty of bad ones.

Her eyes narrowed again as if she was weighing his words. Then she frowned. Signing him up wasn't looking good.

Grasping at straws, Jace offered, "I could trade fixes around your house for sessions. Our hourly rates are similar, and, well, if no money is exchanged, then I'm not really a client. Not on your books, at least."

"Sessions under the table?"

"My services for yours. We'll be helping each other. No harm, no foul."

Meredith shook her head, but her lips curled into a smile. "You're persuasive, I'll give you that, but I'm not taking you on as a client."

Disappointment settled in his belly as he finished his drink and rose to leave. "Just think about it."

Meredith stood, too. She deposited both glasses in the deep sink and waited for him to go. It wasn't his place to stay and she didn't appear to want him to. Funny, he wanted to stay. It was Friday evening, but she probably had plans—

"Jace?"

He was nearly through her door, and turned. "Yeah?"

"I spoke with Tommy's mother. She doesn't mind you observing her son's next therapy session, so maybe we can start there. A volunteer basis only."

Jace cocked his head to the side. "The twelve-year-old?"

"Yes."

Jace wasn't sure he wanted to share things in front of a kid, but maybe it didn't work that way. Maybe it was about telling the horse. That, he could definitely do. "Count me in."

"We'll talk more Monday."

Jace turned, toolbox in hand, but paused when he considered how late in the game she'd given him that information. "Why didn't you tell me about observing Tommy's session earlier?"

Meredith looked caught and gave him a sheepish expression. "I wanted to see how you did on the trail ride first."

"Huh." She'd tested him. "I guess I passed then."

"You did. You're much more comfortable around the horses now."

"I am. Have a good weekend."

"You, too, and thanks for fixing my faucet."

"It's what I do." Jace grinned and left.

He whistled on his way to the truck, feeling a little lighter having finally admitted his shortcoming. If Meredith wouldn't take him on as a client, maybe observing her program could help unlock his guarded soul. If nothing else, he could at least get behind her program in this community.

The following Tuesday, Meredith pulled into her driveway, thrilled with the progress on the arena. The steel beams were all in place, and the crew was still working. She checked her watch. It was well after five. She watched a little longer and realized they were wrapping things up. Good. She had her young client, Tommy, coming at seven o'clock and Jace would join them.

In hindsight, she was glad she'd gone out on a limb to ask Tommy's mom about Jace observing. It had worked in their favor, as if he really was seeing how the arena would be used. Still, she'd have to let Sue know that Jace had volunteered to help. She wasn't an ends-justified-the-means sort of person, but having Jace in on Tommy's session might turn out to be a good thing.

She had an idea of what Jace could do this evening, but needed to run it by him first. She went inside to quickly change her clothes. With Jace sticking around, they both needed to eat, so she planned on making sandwiches. She was just finishing up a turkey-and-Swiss for herself when she heard a knock on her kitchen door.

Jace popped his head in. "Hi."

"Come in and tell me what you want on your sandwich. Do you like turkey or ham?"

He grinned. "Either or both with mayo and anything else you'd like to put on it."

Meredith smiled. "Lettuce, tomato and Swiss?"

"Sounds perfect. Can I do something to help?"

She pointed at the basket on top of her refrigerator. "Grab the chips up there and whatever you want to drink from inside the fridge. I have pop, lemonade, milk or water."

Jace nodded and gathered up the items including a jar of pickles, which he placed on the island. "What would you like to drink?"

"Water is fine for me." It was an informal meal and certainly nothing special, but Jace seemed to fill up her kitchen with his presence and he knocked her off-kilter with that smile of his.

Meredith set out paper plates along with the tray of sandwiches. She'd made three and cut them in half, so Jace could help himself to more than one if he wanted. She'd be fortunate to eat a whole sandwich, considering the jitters in her belly.

"So," Jace said as he dumped a pile of chips on his plate. "What should I do while you're working with Tommy?"

"I'm glad you asked. I was hoping that you wouldn't mind going through the exercises with Bella right along with Tommy and Pete. That way, Tommy won't feel like you're watching him. It may help him participate if he sees you going through the motions, too."

Jace grabbed two sandwich halves. "Okay, sure, but you're not going to ask me to confess my darkest secrets or anything, are you?"

Meredith saw the mischievous look in his eyes and blurted out, "How many do you have?"

"None that I care to repeat in front of a twelve-year-old." Jace winked at her, as if they were the ones sharing a secret.

Meredith sucked in a breath. She was in way

over her head when it came to Jace Moore. No wonder he had a reputation. The guy could tease with charm. She was glad that she'd refused him as a client, and hoped she didn't regret allowing him to volunteer.

Forcing herself back on track, she said, "Equine therapy is not like that. I give out a series of easy activities with the intent that you'll share your secrets with the horse."

"But Bella might not like what I have to say." Again, he refused to be serious.

"Look, Jace. No jokes with Tommy today, okay? He needs to—"

Jace had raised his hand. "I'm just playing with you. I get this is important and I'll do whatever you want me to."

Her cheeks grew warm. She wasn't used to being teased. Not since she was kid, anyway, and especially not by an attractive man sitting in her kitchen, eating sandwiches like it was the most ordinary thing in the world. It *was* ordinary, but not for her. "Okay, great. Thanks."

Jace raised his sandwich. "No, thank you. These are great, by the way."

"A simple sandwich."

"Made with care, and I appreciate it."

Now, he was serious, and that wasn't any better. Nope, much worse. He made her feel like she'd brought down the moon and slapped it on the plate for him. "You're welcome."

Meredith took a deep breath and hoped Jace's presence tonight might help Tommy relax. It could also have the opposite effect, and then that would be the end of Jace's *volunteering*.

"So after this we feed the horses, then wait for the kid to show up?"

"I need to lay down some cones in the outdoor arena. You can help with those if you'd like to."

"Cones?"

"I was encouraged by Tommy reaching out to Pete. Tonight, we'll start with grooming, and if that goes well and Tommy isn't afraid, then I'd like to take the horses to the outdoor arena for a walk around the cones. You will guide Bella, and Tommy will guide Pete. I'll be right there, of course."

"Interesting. And this will help the kid?"

"That's the goal. Tommy has trust issues since his father left. He's afraid the horses will hurt him—so my hope is to show him that the horses are afraid, too. They're not sure if you and Tommy will hurt them. We'll build from there."

Jace listened with an intensity in his gaze as if she might be describing him. But then his expression cleared and he polished off the last of his chips and pickles. He downed his root beer, and stood with his plate in hand. "Let's do this."

Meredith took their plates and tossed them in the trash. Then she wrapped up the leftover sandwich half that she didn't touch, while Jace returned the jar of pickles to the fridge. It was equal parts comfort and discomfort moving around her kitchen with him. At one point, her arm brushed his as they both reached to push the stools in under the ledge of the island. Skin on skin sent a shiver up her spine, but glancing at Jace, he seemed unmoved.

Meredith squared her shoulders before opening the door. "Remember, everything that happens in session, stays in session. This is confidential stuff. And you're here as a volunteer who's observing."

"Of course." And Jace gave her that grin that knocked her a little loopy. The smile she liked seeing far too much.

Standing next to Meredith, Jace watched her twelve-year-old client make his way toward them, shuffling alongside his mom. The kid wasn't very tall and a little thick around the middle. His tennis shoes were untied and his hair mussed.

"Hi, Tommy," Meredith said.

The kid mumbled something, but Jace couldn't tell what. If he'd been the kid's parent, he wouldn't let him get away with such a rude greeting. He remembered that his older brother had never let him or Jeremy look away from someone speaking to them. John would have given them an earful afterwards, if they'd acted like this kid.

"Sue, this is Jace Moore, my builder. As we discussed, he's here to observe how the arena will be used. And depending on Tommy, possibly volunteer in future sessions if you're okay with that."

Jace reached out his hand toward the mom, who gave him too broad of a smile. "Nice to meet to you."

"And you, too. Of course, I'm good with whatever helps Tommy." Sue returned his handshake and held on a couple of seconds too long.

Seriously? This woman was casting out signals he had no intention of picking up.

"Then, let's head for the stable." Meredith turned toward Sue. "Feel free to relax outside or come back in an hour and a half. Whatever you're most comfortable with."

Jace saw the brief flash of disappointment replaced by a smile. "I'll be back. If I stick around, I might hover like I did last time."

Meredith nodded. "Thank you for that. See you soon."

Jace noticed the kid dragged his feet and fell behind them. With his voice low, he asked, "So the parents really don't watch?"

"Not after the first session. Having them present often stifles the interaction. They need to remain out of earshot or not at all."

Relieved that Tommy's mom wouldn't be hanging around, Jace slipped inside the stable with Meredith. The smells of fresh hay and warm horses wrapped around Jace as they waited for Tommy to catch up. They were familiar scents now—sweet and earthy. Ever since he'd first helped Meredith feed her horses, this was something he looked forward to at the end of his day. Maybe these sessions would be similar, but right now his gut tensed. Meredith had refused to take him on as a client, but she'd made a way for him to legitimately observe and volunteer. Would any of that actually help him?

Together, Jace and Meredith led both Pete and Bella into the open area of the stable, then looped their lead ropes into hooks on the walls in preparation for brushing. Jace noticed that Tommy looked pretty scared as he approached Pete.

"I was nervous, too, the first couple of times I was around the horses," Jace said softly.

Tommy glanced at him with wide, forlorn-looking brown eyes.

Jace regretted his initial irritation with Tommy as it was obvious the kid had been deeply hurt. Jace remembered how lost he'd felt after his parents had died. His whole world had been upended. Not unlike this kid, whose father had left. Did he ever see his dad? Why a man would leave his kid in such turmoil was beyond Jace.

Meredith handed each of them a curry comb. "We're going to start with brushing the horses and see how it goes. It's okay if you're nervous—the horses are, too. They don't know if you're going to be kind or not. Just take your time and the more you relax, the more they will as well. They pick up cues from you and respond accordingly."

Jace looked forward to brushing Bella. He'd enjoyed it after his first ride, but this seemed different. This was supposed to be *therapy*, so he concentrated on long, even strokes with the comb.

He hoped to ride again, maybe this week if Meredith had time. She hadn't been joking about needing to build up to longer rides. He'd woken up with soreness in muscles he didn't even know he had. He'd walked a little bow-legged for a day, but he was ready to get back in the saddle as soon as Meredith said the word.

He glanced at the kid. Tommy brushed Pete with short, tentative strokes, so Jace switched to Bella's other side so the kid could see how he was doing it. Sure enough, Tommy watched him a minute then drew out his strokes a little longer. Pete responded with a gentle whicker that made Tommy smile.

"Like that, huh?" Tommy whispered to the horse. "I wish you could talk."

What would Pete say, if he could? Jace wondered what Bella might say to him. Would she scold him for considering women as pleasant distractions? The time spent with them was a way to forget what he'd lost if only for a couple of hours. He knew his mother would disapprove of the way he'd lived most of his adult life. It shamed him to even think about what she might say.

"Probably you, too, huh, girl?" Jace murmured. He brushed Bella's mane until the thick strands felt softer to his fingers. The memory of his mom laughing when he wouldn't sit still while she cut his hair washed over him like a tidal wave followed by the usual ache that pierced his chest when he remembered her. Raising three boys, his mother had had patience by the truckload. And they'd all pushed that patience far too many times.

Jace stilled the brushing and briefly closed his eyes. *I miss her, Lord. I miss them both. Why'd You take them?*

When he opened his eyes, his gaze connected with Meredith's. He read concern in the softening of those sky-blue eyes that held him hostage for a few seconds before he looked away.

Meredith stood next to Tommy, showing the kid where to put hair from Pete's mane that clogged up the curry comb. The boy had copied him in brushing his horse's mane. *That was good, right?*

They brushed both horses until their backs practically gleamed, and so far, very little had been said. Although, Jace felt a sense of peace in that silence as if he'd verbally expressed to Bella how much he missed his parents and the horse had understood. Jace wasn't sharing his darkest secrets no matter how much he'd joked around about it, but this was a start.

"Tommy," Meredith said. "Would you like to take Pete for a walk to the outdoor arena?"

Jace watched as fear flashed in the kid's eyes again. He couldn't help but speak up. "I'll be out there, too, walking Bella."

Meredith gave him a look before focusing back on Tommy. "Whatever you want to do, okay?"

He'd overstepped his *observer* role, but really, how long could they just stand here and keep brushing? Surely the kid was bored with that. But, of course, he wasn't. Tommy continued to brush Pete like he couldn't help himself. Like it was calming some deep recesses of his soul. The boy's eyes weren't so forlorn now. Jace glanced back at Meredith, but she was concentrating on Tommy.

"Take your time," she said. "We can brush Pete for as long as you like. He enjoys it and he doesn't get brushed nearly enough."

"I like it," Tommy said.

"Why's that?" Meredith asked.

Jace hung on hearing the answer.

Tommy shrugged. "I don't know. It makes me feel better."

Smart kid. Jace wanted to rush onto the next thing or the next woman. Especially after memories took him by surprise. He typically ran from them, busied himself with something, anything that kept him from feeling that deep sense of loss.

Jace continued long strokes with the curry comb along Bella's haunches. Maybe he should revisit those memories of how his mom used to cut his hair. Jeremy's and John's, too. They were good times. Their mom used to take the clippers to their dad's unruly dark locks as well, when she could catch him. Their dad used to go months and months between haircuts. And they used to marvel at how much hair had puddled on the kitchen floor.

Maybe missing those times was okay. Maybe working through the pain those memories stirred was okay, too. If nothing else, reminiscing felt a little like honoring his parents instead of shutting them out.

Chapter Five

Meredith waved goodbye to Tommy and his mom. Tonight's session had gone really well. The boy had opened up a little more when they broke away from Jace in order to process the takeaways from tonight's session in private.

She'd asked Tommy if he wanted Jace to volunteer in future sessions and wasn't surprised when the boy stated that he hoped Jace would be there. Having Jace in attendance, doing the same things as Tommy, had helped the boy venture out instead of staying withdrawn and fearful. Jace had made a big difference because Tommy craved male attention and approval.

She turned to Jace. "Thank you for being chill tonight. Your presence with Bella helped Tommy a lot. You did well not to make him feel watched or on the spot."

He smiled. "I didn't do much, but I can do it again next week and any week you need me."

"That would be awesome. And Tommy will appreciate it, too." Meredith couldn't help but rationalize that Jace was truly volunteering even though he was going through the exercises as well. Still, it made her feel like she was walking a tightrope of ethics. One misstep and—

"So what's with Tommy's mom?"

"Sue? Why?" Surely, Jace wasn't agreeing to come next week in order to see Sue. Had he taken an interest in her?

Sue's gaze had strayed to Jace more than a few times, but no surprise there. Jace was attractive and Sue was a pretty woman who'd been hurt. Why she'd try to venture back onto the playing field so soon was beyond Meredith. And why did she care if Jace was interested in her client's mom? She shouldn't, although it wasn't a good idea, all things considered.

Jace shrugged. "I don't know. Is she like stable? Tommy sure seems lost."

"I'm sure she's doing the best she can." Meredith led the horses out into the pasture.

Tommy was *a lot* lost, but Meredith wasn't going to share details that were too confidential. Their session had never moved beyond the stable, but that was okay. Tommy needed to brush Pete for the entire time. He was working through pain and Meredith believed Jace was, too.

When he'd looked at her with those anguish-filled eyes, she'd been hard-pressed not to go to him and help draw out his grief, but she'd remained focused on Tommy. The boy was her client, and Jace, well, she was still trying to come to grips with their arrangement, hoping she'd made the right decision.

"I'm going to pick up those cones. We might use them next week." Meredith grabbed a large basket and walked toward the outdoor arena.

"I'll help you." Jace followed her. "Do you want the stable door closed?"

"Nah. It's fine until we leave." Meredith bent to pick up the soft, colorful cones. They were smaller than the ones used for roadwork and much easier to place for clients to guide the horses around.

As Jace walked toward the second set of cones they'd placed in a line, Bella came close to the pasture fence and watched them.

Meredith couldn't help but chuckle. "She's got her eye on you."

Jace flashed a grin.

And Meredith shook her head. Even her mare was captivated by the man.

"Have you considered having a grand opening for the indoor arena once it's completed?" Jace handed her the stack of cones he'd collected.

"I have, but it depends on when you'll be done."

Jace nodded. "How's the third full weekend in September sound? The following weekend is the Elk Festival, so we don't want to compete with that."

"We?"

"Considering I'm a volunteer here, I could help

out with your grand opening." Jace gave her another of his stellar smiles.

Meredith felt a zip of anticipation course through her veins. His help would be welcome, but was it wise? She already had Liza's promise to help. How would that work with the two of them? She'd told her friend that Jace was spearheading the arena, but Meredith hadn't mentioned anything about him *volunteering*.

"We've got a date to shoot for, at least. What ideas do you have for the big day?" Jace wasn't letting this go.

"Other than introducing my program, I was thinking along the lines of an open house. Hot dogs and face painting and such."

Jace nodded. "What about fundraising?"

Meredith grimaced. "Wouldn't that seem a little pushy?"

"Not if you did it right. You could have an auction. People love that sort of thing."

"Auction what?"

He snapped his fingers. "Community services. We could get the businesses in Rose River to donate something people can bid on."

Meredith's eyes widened. It was a great idea, but again, Jace was including himself. "We?"

"I've known some of these folks my whole life. It'd be a piece of cake for me to ask for a donation."

She couldn't argue with that. She'd been thinking about how she wanted to showcase her program to the community and if this went well, it could be an annual thing. Fundraising could be part of that, too. "Definitely something to consider and any donation would be tax-deductible, of course. Wow, I really appreciate your ideas. Thanks."

They entered the stable and Meredith set the basket of cones in the tack room, where she had an area designated for therapy exercise equipment and toys. She turned to find Jace watching from the doorway. It made her belly do a flip-flop.

"Your program is going to be a hit, Miss Lewis."

Warmth filled her, but there was a gleam in his eyes. What was he up to? "What makes you say that?"

"You keep your stable clean and organized. Your therapy sessions are different than I expected, I'll give you that, but helpful. Tommy walked away with a smile tonight. Auctioning off services from the community is a win-win, starting with Three Sons Construction. I'll check with John about what we might donate."

"Thank you." Meredith smiled, but inside she battled disappointment. Of course, he was in this to grow his business, too.

"So now that we have the date and an auction idea, what else would you like to include?"

Meredith got back to business. Despite her reservations, she wasn't going to turn down his help.

She'd make good use of his willingness to be a volunteer. "Do you have time to come in and go over my notes?"

"Of course." He gestured for her to lead the way.

They walked toward the house as the sun was setting beyond them. The trees around her property took on a stunning rose-orange hue, making Meredith stop in her tracks.

"What's wrong?" Jace asked as he turned toward her.

"Nothing. Just look at that sky."

"Ah, yeah, sure. It's lovely."

She glanced at him. Who said *lovely* anymore? But he didn't look too impressed with the colors of the fading sunlight. He seemed to be watching her. "What?"

He reached out and lifted one of her two braids. "For a moment there, your hair caught fire in the sunlight."

Her mouth opened but nothing came out. Was that a compliment or a simple observation? Her mop of kinky red hair was the second bane of her existence, right after her freckles. She could tame her hair by braiding it; the freckles were a lost cause.

He still held her braid, inspecting it. "Do you ever wear it loose?"

Meredith backed away quick with a nervous chuckle and her braided pigtail left his grasp. "Rarely. It's a tangled mess. I have pictures of me as a kid with a bob haircut that was more like a frizzy ring around my head. So, no, I don't wear it down."

He gave her a crooked half grin that made her heart race. "Too bad."

Was he flirting?

Meredith couldn't be sure. Guys like him didn't flirt with girls like her, but for a moment… She shook off the thought. She wasn't going there. Not ever. She couldn't.

Jace seemed to snap out of whatever had made him consider her hair in the rays of the setting sun. "Let's see what you have in your notes."

Jace followed Meredith into her kitchen. What had he been thinking to touch her hair that way?

"Want something to drink?" she asked without looking at him. In fact, she hurried around the kitchen as if she wanted to get him in and back out fast.

Just look at her notes and go. "I'd love some of that lemonade."

"Sure thing." Meredith poured him a glass.

"Nothing for you?"

"Nope, I'm good." She dashed into the dining room. "My arena notebook is in here."

He made his way toward her, but leaned against the entrance, sipping lemonade as he watched her pull a red three-ring binder from a book bag sitting next to her laptop. She was definitely organized—always jotting down notes and making plans. Did she ever do anything spur-of-the-moment? She had allowed him in on Tommy's session, but even that had been cleared ahead of time with the kid's mom. Obviously, Meredith had weighed the pros and cons of his presence and he'd come out on top.

He stepped forward just as she turned around, and he bumped right into her. He cupped her elbow with his free hand. "Sorry."

Meredith's cheeks looked as red as her hair, but she managed to pull out a chair and perched on the edge like a rabbit ready to dash away if he made any fast moves.

He pulled his chair closer to hers to see what she had in her notes and Meredith's cheeks flamed again. He nearly laughed, but didn't. Ever since he'd touched her braid, she'd acted jittery, like he made her nervous. He was king at the art of making women feel at ease, so where was that superpower now? "Show me what you've got."

Still not looking at him, she opened the folder. "I was thinking about an autumn-festival vibe with tours of the stable."

"You could have testimonials from past clients posted on the walls with pictures if that's allowed. People need to not only see the impact your program has, but understand it, too."

"That's a great idea." Meredith didn't look at him, though.

"Of course, it is." He hoped a little teasing might get them back on normal footing.

She finally looked up and laughed.

Success.

"I'll contact my prior clients and see if they'd be willing to do that."

"We could get a local band to play. My brother Jeremy has a friend in a country band. They're always looking for exposure. I'll look into it."

Meredith's eyes went wide. "You're turning out to be a good volunteer. That'd be great."

Something about the huskiness in her voice paired with the surprise in those baby blues hit him like a two-by-four between the eyes, making him blink rapidly. Now, *he* was nervous.

Jace stood quickly and pushed in the chair. "Sounds like we have a plan. Might as well reconvene next week, after Tommy's session. I could have a few donations lined up by then."

Meredith stood, too. "Great."

Jace drained the rest of his lemonade. "Thanks for this. I'll put it in the sink on my way out. See you tomorrow, then."

"See you tomorrow." Meredith remained standing in the dining room.

Jace picked up his pace as he left Meredith's. He jogged down the steps and even across the gravel driveway. Once in his truck, he ran his hand down over his mouth. What had just happened in there? He'd been aware of Meredith on a completely different level. Attraction had sizzled between them and that was something new. And complicated and wrong…for both of them.

Sunday mornings at the Moore house were pretty relaxed and today was no different. Jace enjoyed having breakfast with his brothers before heading off to church. It had become something of a new tradition, since during the week they were often going in different directions and didn't have time for a sit-down morning meal.

"I'll drive if you guys are ready," John offered.

Jace rinsed his plate and put it in the dishwasher. "That works."

Jeremy finished his coffee. "Yeah, I'm ready to go after I let the dog out."

Molly was still licking Jeremy's plate on the floor under the table.

"Come on, Mol." The dog followed Jeremy outside.

"I'll be in the truck." John stood, petting Henry, who swirled his legs and mewed for something. John scooped up the cat and put him outside as he left, letting the screen door shut with a snap. Their other cat, Snowball, came running once she heard the door opened, but John was gone.

Jace opened it for Snowball, then loaded Jeremy's plate in the dishwasher before following his brothers.

Once outside, he felt the hot sun on his shoulders. It was the last Sunday in August and Labor Day weekend loomed the following week. Hopefully, he could get outdoors for something fun. Riding horses with Meredith instantly came to mind.

She'd popped into his thoughts more times than he cared to contemplate. It had all started with thoughts of unbraiding her hair after Tommy's session. That awareness had only increased while he'd sat next to her in her dining room. He'd been careful to keep his distance since then, not standing too close. She was a client. And he was a volunteer. He wouldn't impinge on her code of ethics.

After slipping into the passenger side of John's crew-cab truck, Jace glanced at Jeremy sprawled on the back seat. "You could have rode shotgun."

Jeremy shrugged. "Didn't care to."

Rose River might be a small town, but there were several churches. Jace and Jeremy went where John attended—a community chapel outside of town.

On the short drive, Jace figured now was as good a time as any to bring up the silent auction. "Meredith Lewis plans to have a grand opening event for the riding arena when it's complete. I'm helping her with it and think we should donate the cost of our labor for a silent auction."

"What kind of job are you thinking?" John asked.

Jace had thought this one over. "How about the labor on a roof replacement? A one-day job. We can put a limit on the size of the roof. Something along those lines."

"And why are we doing this?" John asked.

"It's good marketing, for one. And two, this is a good program to get behind. I'm hoping our commitment will push the community to embrace her nonprofit."

"Doesn't she advertise?" Jeremy asked.

"Not without the finished arena. She needs the indoor space to grow," Jace clarified.

"What do you think?" John asked their younger brother, glancing at him in the back through the rearview mirror.

"I'm fine with it."

"Consider it done." John nodded. "We can figure out the parameters as we get closer."

"Good. Thanks." Jace relaxed.

"You're really into this woman," Jeremy stated with awe as if Jace wasn't capable of anything deep, or lasting.

Both were true. Still, Jace felt his shoulders tense. "I'm into her program and the horses really do make a difference for people."

Including him. There was something freeing in letting down his guard when he was around those horses, especially Bella. Jace didn't feel like he had to plaster on his happy face. He could slow down and just be.

"Uh-huh," Jeremy teased. "You're spending a lot of time over there."

"I like horses." Jace took every opportunity he could to be around them. It couldn't be about the woman who owned them. But Meredith calmed him as well, until awareness of her had kicked in and hit him over the head. He had to keep a professional, friendly distance until that arena was complete. Until he was more complete inside as well.

"So what's this paragon of good works look like?" Jeremy asked.

"What does that matter?" Jace bristled.

"Lay off him, Jer. Meredith Lewis is a client." John's softspoken command held weight and they both settled down.

As they pulled into the church parking lot, Jace tried to shake off his brother's taunts, but there was no denying that he found Meredith attractive. He wasn't ready for the kind of relationship she would require. Meredith wasn't a casual sort of woman, and he couldn't handle a serious entanglement. He had few options other than a professional friendship where she was concerned.

He entered the prefabricated building with its simple facade of a wooden cross attached to the side that faced the road—the only thing that identified the modular-home look-alike as a church.

"Hi, Jace, how've you been?"

He turned to see Liza Smith, a woman he'd

gone on a few dates with before he'd fully surrendered to faith in God. It hadn't worked with Liza—she was looking for more than he could give. "I'm good. How about you?"

She smiled, showing off white teeth against a nice summer tan. As a grade school teacher, Liza had summers off, and by the looks of it, she'd been enjoying her break. "I hear you're building an arena for a friend of mine."

A sinking feeling settled in his midsection. Liza was friends with Meredith—great, just great. He played dumb. "Yeah?"

"Yeah. Meredith Lewis. Be good to her, you hear?"

"She's a client." This was the second time this morning he'd had to defend his relationship with Meredith. He wasn't looking to carelessly date her. He liked Meredith far too much. Besides, he wasn't that guy anymore.

Liza gave him a pointed look as if she'd read his thoughts. "And a kind woman."

"Of course." What else could he say? Did Meredith know he'd dated Liza? He let out a sigh. If they were friends, then probably. And most likely, Liza had told Meredith how he was a jerk for leaving her in the lurch.

The song service started and Jace took his usual place near the back alongside John and Jeremy. John had come to this church since shortly after their parents had died. And although Jace and

Jeremy's attendance over the years, and even recently, had been spotty at best, John had never wavered in his commitment to God or this congregation.

He glanced at Liza, who always sat up front. At that same moment, she turned and caught his gaze. He gave her a nod, which she returned with a cautious smile, making him wonder what she had told Meredith about him.

Chapter Six

Meredith rose from her seat at an outdoor table to wave over her friend. They had a lot of catching up to do. She'd made plans to meet Liza for lunch at the Rose River Café after their respective church services. Although, Meredith's church let out much earlier than Liza's.

"I hope you don't mind sitting outside. I know it's really hot today."

Liza gave her a hug. "Are you kidding? We have to enjoy every bit of summer while we can. Those cooler days are right around the corner."

Meredith laughed. "And you go back to school soon."

Liza nodded. "This week. But we have Friday off before Labor Day weekend, so that's a nice break."

Meredith worked on Friday, but would knock off early. Most of her coworkers did. She looked forward to a three-day weekend, but hadn't made any plans. "What are you doing for Labor Day?"

Liza shrugged. "The usual. Going up to my parents' cabin. The whole family will be there, but there's plenty of room. Would you like to go with me?"

"Not sure I could get away for the entire weekend." The horses would be okay for a couple of days, but she didn't like leaving them for more than that.

"Come for whatever amount of time you can. We have a huge cookout on Labor Day and we can lounge on the beach."

Meredith had been up there once. Liza's family cabin was situated east of Cheboygan, right on Lake Huron, with access to miles of glorious, sandy beach. "Maybe I will. Can I let you know?"

"Sure, sure. No pressure. You could text me the day of or just show up."

Meredith smiled. "Thanks, Liza. You're awesome."

"Of course."

The waitress came with water and menus, apologized for the wait, promised to be right back and darted away. The place was busy and the outdoor patio was packed. And no wonder, with a pretty view overlooking the Rose River, from which the town got its name. Clumps of pink-rose bushes grew wild along the banks.

Meredith opened up her menu and decided on a big salad with grilled chicken on top. "What are you having?"

"Hmm, I'm pretty boring. Probably a burger and fries."

Liza was anything but. She was a dark-haired beauty with a robust laugh that matched her big heart. "Guess who I saw at my church this morning?"

Meredith cocked her head. "Who?"

Liza's dark eyes shone. "Jace Moore."

"So he really does go to church."

"Yeah, sometimes. It's how we met, but I haven't seen him there in months, until recently."

Meredith felt a skitter of unease run up her spine. Would Jace get interested in Liza now that he was back in attendance? Church was important to her friend and that twinkle in her eye definitely looked positive.

"Meredith?" Liza looked concerned.

"Sorry, my thoughts wandered. Good for him for going back to church."

Her friend tipped her head. "How's he doing with the arena?"

"Great. He loves the horses, especially Bella." She wouldn't expose their special connection. "He often helps feed them after his workday. He's sort of a volunteer."

"Nice."

"Yeah." Meredith didn't want to get too specific about how Jace volunteered. That was probably better left alone. For now.

"Just be careful."

"Why?" Meredith asked with a laugh.

"He's a, you know, love-'em-and-leave-'em type. A heartbreaker if you let him."

"Like he broke yours?" The words were out before she could catch them, but Meredith had consoled her friend over tubs of gourmet ice cream after Jace had dumped her. It was old news.

Liza shook her head. "I let him sweep me off my feet and maybe hoped for things that weren't there, but in hindsight, he's about this deep." She made a gesture of a couple of inches with her thumb and forefinger.

"Don't worry, he's not the least bit interested in me." Meredith wasn't about to enlighten her friend that she believed Jace ran much deeper.

Given the loss of his parents and the emotional debts he felt he owed his older brother, Meredith would say Jace made a concerted effort to appear like a shallow pond. Seemingly superficial, but there were ripples in Jace that hinted at very deep waters beneath. Troubled waters that Bella had sensed.

"Don't be so sure that he's not," Liza said.

"Yeah, right." Meredith laughed a little too quickly. There was that moment at the dining room table when Jace had sat too close. And he'd wanted to see her hair undone…

"Seriously." Liza touched her forearm. "Be careful."

Just then, the waitress reappeared and took their orders. A welcome reprieve. Meredith didn't like keeping things from her friend, but she didn't want to share Jace's reasons for *volunteering*. Liza was a local teacher and Meredith had repeatedly tried to get her program in front of the school counselor. If Liza presented Jace's involvement incorrectly, it could come back to bite Meredith in the worst way.

She drained her water glass, then asked, "Do you remember his parents?"

Liza made a face. "Not really. I was only twelve when they were killed. I was in many of Jeremy's classes and I remember when the teacher announced the tragedy. It was a couple of weeks before Jeremy came back to school, but he was definitely a different kid. Angry."

Meredith knew the impact such a devastating event could have on teens. She'd had her own crisis when her parents split. It's why she went into counseling and Bella was the reason she specialized in equine therapy. "Stuff like that stays with a person regardless of how well or unwell they handle it."

Liza narrowed her gaze. "You think maybe Jace is still dealing with the loss of his parents?"

"I'm sure they all have their moments." Meredith wasn't going to divulge any information that Jace had confided. It wasn't her place to tell.

What Jace had told her about him and his brothers going away from the house for Christmas showed how difficult they found the holidays.

Even though the brothers had stuck together, they were a broken family missing the two most important people.

"Huh, I suppose you're right." Liza sat back as if that reality had never dawned on her before. "I suppose I should give Jace a little slack."

Maybe Liza's heart had been more bruised than broken. Meredith couldn't blame her. It'd be easy to get swept away by Jace's charm. With him volunteering, now more than ever, she needed to keep her guard up and maintain a friendly distance from the guy. His reputation was real, and regardless of the reasons behind it, Meredith didn't want her heart bruised or broken.

Jace pulled up in front of the Rose River Café and parked. It wasn't the fanciest restaurant in town, but it was one of the best. He'd spoken to the owner about donating a gift certificate for Meredith's silent auction and wanted to pick it up before he forgot about it or they did. The place was busy with the after-church crowd, but he wasn't here to eat, not when his pancake breakfast still weighed heavy in his stomach. He'd pick up the certificate and then head for the hardware store.

He got out of his truck and walked toward the entrance of the café just as two women were exiting. Meredith. And Liza. *Nice.* He smiled. "Hello, ladies."

Meredith's eyes widened. "Hi, Jace."

He admired the summery blue dress Meredith
was wearing with one long glance. The color
made her eyes pop. He lingered mere seconds on
her bare shoulders, dotted with the same rose-gold
freckles as her face. He wanted to trace a line with
his fingertips from her cheeks to her shoulders,
connecting the dots. But that was as impossible
as it was wrong.

He'd been staring *way* too long. Running his
hand through his hair, he offered an awkward
explanation, "Sorry, not used to seeing you in a
dress."

Meredith raised one red eyebrow.

That didn't come out right even if it was true.
He'd only seen Meredith in jeans and T-shirts.
Even her work outfits were simple pants and tops.
It was jarring to see her wear something so femi-
nine, so pretty, and it suddenly seemed really hot
standing on the sidewalk.

"I've got to go. See ya, Jace." Liza patted Meredith's arm. "Call me later?"

"I will." Meredith didn't meet his gaze and her
cheeks were rosy. So was her nose. She looked
cute with a little sunburn. "So…what's up?"

He gave himself a mental shake. What *was* he
here for? "Um, yeah. I'm picking up a gift certificate for the silent auction."

She waved at Liza, who beeped the car's horn
as she drove by. "That's great. Thank you."

"I know Sunday's probably not the best day to

do this, but would you care to join me? I'm going to the hardware store. They promised a donation, too, and it'd be nice to introduce you to Sam, the owner. Then we can hit some other places."

Her eyes looked cautious, wary even, but she nodded. "Sure. I've made a couple of calls, but haven't heard back from anyone yet. The bakery and the auto shop where I take my truck."

"I checked with my brothers and we'll donate a full day's labor on a roof."

"Wow. Are you sure? That's like, huge."

He chuckled, knowing she'd be grateful but enjoying her surprise even more. "Yes. We're sure. Let me grab the gift certificate and I'll be right back."

Meredith nodded. "I'll be here."

Something about that statement ping-ponged deep inside of him. It was an odd feeling that made his pulse skip a beat. Would she really be there for him? For always?

He shook his head once again, trying to clear it. He'd seen beautiful women in alluring clothes before, but the effect of a simple blue sundress seemed to be knocking him for a loop.

After slipping inside the restaurant, he told the hostess what he was there for and she made him wait for a moment while she checked in the back.

Tapping his fingers on the hostess station, he glanced out the glass windows overlooking Main Street. Meredith had turned and he could see freckles sprinkled along her back. Like soft confetti. She had twined her usual long braid into a circle at the back of her head, making her neck look long. Graceful.

"Here you go, sir." The hostess handed him an envelope.

"Thanks." He peeked at the amount and smiled as he exited the café. Then he showed Meredith. "There's two dinners covered in here."

"Yay! That's really nice."

"Yeah." He'd never been this clumsy around a woman before. One blue dress turned him into a tongue-tied teen who didn't know how to act. That was so not him. "Let's head for the hardware store."

"Lead the way."

"Right." He glanced at her walking beside him and noticed that her eyelashes were darker, too.

"*What* are you looking at?"

"I don't know. Not used to you in a dress."

Meredith chuckled. "You said that already."

"It's true, I didn't expect—"

"Me to dress like a girl?" Meredith gazed at him with merry blue eyes. She was mocking him alright, and enjoying every minute of his discomfort.

He didn't expect her to look this *good* dressed like a girl. But no way could he say that. She didn't like compliments, and she might take it the wrong way, as if he'd added a dig in there, too. "Sorry, forget I said anything."

She waved her hand in dismissal. "Okay. Forgotten."

They walked along the sidewalk of downtown Rose River until they reached the hardware store at the end of the sidewalk. Once inside, the overly air-conditioned interior sent a chill through him. He glanced at Meredith and she rubbed her bare arms.

"You can wait outside if you're cold."

"I'll be fine."

"How can I help...? Oh, hello, Jace. What brings you in?"

Jace had known the owner of the hardware store his whole life. Sam had been friends with his dad. "We talked about a store gift card for a donation to a silent auction. This is Meredith Lewis, who runs RR Equine Therapy."

"Oh, yeah. Tell me again, what's this for?"

Meredith stepped forward. "I run a not-for-profit equine therapy program and Three Sons Construction is building my indoor arena. The silent auction is to raise both funds and awareness for the program highlighted at my grand opening."

"Equine therapy? For like the disabled?" Sam looked duly impressed.

Jace was, too. Meredith handled herself well, professionally, but then he didn't expect anything less.

Meredith smiled. "Maybe down the road, but for now it's more emotional or mental therapy.

Post-traumatic stress or trauma. I'm a certified counselor and I work with mostly teens."

Sam glanced at Jace. "Good advertisement for you, too, I suppose."

Jace grinned. "Of course."

"Well, okay then. Let me get one made up. Be back in a minute." Sam dashed into the office and returned with a plastic card that he rang through the register. Then he handed it over to Meredith along with a one-hundred-dollar receipt.

Meredith took it in one hand but reached out to shake Sam's hand with the other. "Thank you. I will send you a donation receipt for tax purposes."

"Great. When's the big day?"

Meredith glanced at Jace.

He nodded. "Not yet confirmed, but we're thinking the Saturday before the Elk Festival. We'll let you know for sure."

"Sounds good."

"Thanks, Sam." Jace turned to leave and opened the door for Meredith.

Once outside, she said, "That was great. But then, everyone's giving because they know you."

"Doesn't matter. After the grand opening, they'll know you, too."

She bit her lip. "I hope they're not disappointed."

"There's no way that will happen." He cupped her elbow, noticing the softness of her skin. "Come on. There's a couple of other shops we can hit."

"Okay."

He let his hand drop away from her, but he couldn't stop thinking about the softness of Meredith's skin and all those freckles.

Monday evening, Meredith pulled into her driveway and smiled at the progress. The building was fully enclosed now and it looked great. Jace and his crew were still working, so she got out of her truck and headed for the work site. She wanted to see the inside and *feel* the space.

The last full weekend in September for the grand opening wasn't out of reach. Not at all. Everything was coming together but a zip of unsettled nerves tingled up her spine. Could she really pull off hosting the community here? The indoor arena was a dream finally come true—one she hoped didn't turn into a nightmare.

She briefly closed her eyes. *God, please don't let me mess this up.*

Yesterday, after the hardware store, she and Jace had gathered up several more donations including one from the owner of a local hair salon who happened to be in her shop when they'd walked by. It was Jace's idea to stop in, and sure enough, she donated a cut with color. The owner knew Jace, and by the way the woman had visually gobbled him up, Meredith wondered if they'd gone out.

Everyone knew Jace and more donations than she could wrangle on her own came in because of it. She'd actually received a few calls today from folks who'd gladly chipped in once they'd heard Three Sons Construction was involved. Her auto repair shop donated a full tune-up.

Meredith slipped into an opening that would become a barn door and marveled at the size of the arena. Oh, she knew the dimensions on paper, but this was perfect. She could easily conduct sessions in here with both horses and have lots of room to spare.

Jace was walking along the interior walls with a man who must be the electrician. She'd seen his van when she'd pulled in. Jace looked up and waved.

She waved back, but didn't intrude. Instead, she looked around the arena, visualizing sessions she could have during the winter months. Glancing up, she saw the openings made for the clear panels under the eaves let in a lot of natural light. She'd still have overhead lighting, but during daylight hours, the arena would be bright. Jace had suggested going big with the few windows she could afford and recommended ones that slid open sideways. They hadn't been installed yet, but their large cardboard boxes leaned against a far wall, along with the two-way glass for the observation booth.

"What do you think?" Jace appeared beside her, smiling.

"It's amazing." She couldn't stop looking around. "And it's going to be nice and bright in here."

"I know. Those clear panels will work well.

Definitely worth the extra." Jace pointed toward the ceiling. "Ventilation will be through the eaves, year-round like you wanted."

Meredith didn't want a heated arena. Her horses were used to the Michigan seasons.

"And that's the booth you wanted off the breezeway to the stable," Jace continued.

Excitement bubbled up inside her. "Thank you."

Jace got a funny look on his face. "You're paying us to do this, remember?"

"Yes, but you listened to what I wanted and made it even better than I imagined it could be."

He flashed her that wide, confident grin. "It's what I do."

And he'd done good. Really good. "What about a kick wall?"

"That will go up last, and I'll have you inspect the start of it, to make sure we get the height and angle right."

"Great." She noticed the guys were finishing up. The electrician, too. "Are you done for the day?"

"I will be soon. Just need to confirm with the electrician when he'll come out to wire for lighting and outlets. Do you need help feeding the horses?"

"No, but if you're free for a short trail ride—"

Jace raised his hand. "Say no more, I'd love to go."

"Good. It's cooler today, so the horses will enjoy picking up the pace a little."

"Count me in."

Meredith smiled. "I'll meet you in the stable after I change clothes."

"Sounds good." His eyes narrowed a little as if he contemplated saying something more, but didn't. He was waved over by one of his crew and took off across the arena at a slow jog.

Meredith watched him a second or two before making her way toward the house, whistling as she went. Once on the trail, they could talk more about the grand opening event. Hopefully, that would help calm her jitters.

On the trail, Jace breathed in the scents of packed earth and woods, and relaxed. He'd texted his brothers not to expect him for dinner. No surprise there, Jace had been missing dinner a lot lately. Birds chirped overhead, while squirrels rustled on the ground, gathering acorns, and the horses each snorted a couple of times as they walked along the path.

"Are you bored, Pete?" Jace murmured as he scratched between the horse's ears.

He'd wanted to try riding Meredith's other horse. Pete was bigger and more suited to his size, and riding him gave Jace a chance to watch Bella interact with her owner. The two moved as one,

having a long history together. And Pete kept trying to take the lead. Jace was okay with that, too.

"Are you ready to go a little faster?" Meredith asked. "There's a nice wide straightaway up
ahead."

"Let's go." He was about to tap his heels against
Pete's side, when Meredith raised her hand to wait.

"Hang on, let me go over a couple of things.
First, we'll start with a trot and as you move into a
cantor you don't post up as much. Be sure to keep
your shoulders in line with your knees and feet.
Pete's great in a cantor and even a gallop. He's
smooth. Bella gets antsy sometimes and dances
around. You'll see."

"Okay." He followed Meredith's lead into a trot
and then after a bit, they were moving faster and
Jace adjusted his movements to go with the horse's
rhythm.

He kept glancing at Meredith to make sure he
was posting up right, but pretty much forgot wor-
rying over his form as he watched hers. Meredith
was a spectacular sight on Bella; her slender body
moved in sync with the horse and her long red
braid and light skin made a stunning contrast to
the dark Arabian.

Pete tried to pass Bella and Meredith reined in
a little to give him room. Like she'd said, Bella
danced around a bit, but fell in behind him and
Pete, and they both let the horses have their way

into a full-on gallop. It was the most exhilarating experience he'd ever had.

When he spotted a narrowing curve in the trail up ahead, Jace reined back a little. "Whoa—whoa, boy."

Pete slowed to a trot then a walk and stopped to shake all over, making Jace laugh, it was so unexpected.

Meredith reined in Bella beside him. "You did great."

Jace grinned. "I felt like a cowboy. And you're right, Pete's a sweet ride. That's the most fun I've ever had."

"Really?" Color fused Meredith's cheeks as she patted Bella's neck.

"Really." He'd meant every word. He loved this.

"Shall we head back?"

"Sure." Jace turned Pete to ride alongside of Meredith and Bella. He could feel a slight hitch in his core and realized horseback riding was more of a workout than he'd imagined. No wonder Meredith stayed thin.

"I've put together a spreadsheet of all the donations for the silent auction. So far, I think we probably have enough. Other than a tour of the arena and stable, meeting the horses and maybe some food, what else is there?" Meredith looked at him. "Have you heard from the band?"

"Jeremy said they are probable. I'll follow up

to make sure. Dancing is a must. There's plenty of room in the arena if they set up there."

"That makes sense, but the sand floor..." She scrunched her nose.

"I can build something for them to stand on. No big deal." She looked like a deer caught in the headlights of a speeding car.

"What?"

She blew out her breath. "I'm not really good in front of a lot of people."

"Don't worry, I can be the MC. I'll use the band's mic."

Her eyes widened. "A master of ceremonies, yes—yes, that's good. Thanks again."

"You're welcome. We just have to lock down the band."

"Won't they want to be paid?"

Jace laughed. "This group? They'd be good with food and drink, but truly, they'll be happy for the exposure. I told Jeremy to consider it a donation."

"I hope you're right about that."

"Leave it to me."

Meredith turned in the saddle to face him and she had a worried look on her face. "Why are you doing all this? I mean, what's in it for you?"

Ouch. Talk about direct. But then, Meredith didn't beat around the bush, or play verbal games. He liked that. "I wasn't kidding when I said it's good publicity for Three Sons Construction."

She tipped her head. "Come on. All this for good word-of-mouth?"

"I'm your volunteer, remember? Okay, yeah, so maybe it's more than just that." Jace wasn't exactly sure why he wanted to help Meredith with her program.

He'd had the urge to look out for her ever since he'd met her, but maybe it went deeper. Jace liked feeling needed and she needed his help with the grand opening.

He blew out his breath. "I like your program and what you're trying to do here. Seeing Tommy smile when I knew his heart was in pieces did something to me. I can relate, I guess, and if working with your horses, connecting with them, helps kids to get beyond what happened to them, then I'm all in."

If he'd had access to a Bella back when he was a teen, would he be different today? Maybe he wouldn't fear opening up his heart. And just maybe, he'd be married by now with kids of his own to love and help grow. His gut twisted with envy at the thought.

Meredith watched him closely, as if weighing the truth of his words. "Are you up for another session with Tommy tomorrow night?"

"Tommy Tuesdays?" Jace asked, glad they were on a different subject, sort of. "Of course."

Meredith chuckled. "Tommy Tuesdays, that's cute. My other two clients come on Thursdays.

But double-duty Thursday doesn't have the same ring."

"No, it doesn't." He chuckled. He wondered what those sessions might be like, but decided he'd stick with Tommy Tuesdays. "Just so you know, I won't be here tomorrow during the day, but the electrician will be. I'm helping my brother on another job site for the day, but I'll be here before Tommy arrives."

"Thanks for the heads-up." Meredith's sky-blue eyes narrowed. "You okay?"

"Just a little stiff here and there." He shifted in the saddle, stretching out his back. He'd been sore the last time they rode and it wasn't nearly as far as they'd gone today. What muscles would complain tomorrow?

Meredith immediately looked remorseful. "We probably shouldn't have gone this far until you're used to it."

"Sometimes the best way to get used to something is to dive right in and do it."

"Is that your philosophy?"

"It is today." Jace's philosophy had always been not to feel too deeply and keep everyone at a distance. Meredith seemed to be slipping past his keep-out signs. Did she even know that? "What about you?"

"What about me?" She looked surprised by the question.

"What made you choose to go into counseling?"

She shrugged. "I'm not good at much else."

"Oh, come on—" But before he could find out more, Meredith clicked her tongue to coax Bella into a trot. Pete joined in, too, and Jace concentrated on posting up, like she'd shown him, as they trotted home.

Muscles he'd never thought about seemed to stretch and pull. He'd be sore tomorrow for sure, but it was worth it. He loved riding and hoped to do more of it.

After dismounting, they walked the horses into the stable. Jace inhaled the sweet scent of horse sweat as he slipped the saddle off Pete. He turned for the tack room when the horse lifted his tail to deposit a pile of manure on the cement with a soft splat.

"You could have waited until you were outside," Jace said to the quarter horse.

Meredith laughed, grabbed a flat-looking shovel and scooped up the muck like it was nothing. She dumped the grassy-smelling manure balls into a wheelbarrow that looked nearly full of the stuff mixed with bits of hay.

"I could have gotten that."

"You're doing so much for me as it is. I can clean up after my horses."

He liked helping her. Looking around the stable, he could get used to horse-related chores. Meredith certainly kept things tidy. He lifted the curry comb, then began brushing Pete, starting at the neck and working his way over the horse's back.

Bella turned her head to look at him as if she wondered why he wasn't brushing her. It made Jace laugh. "Do you think she's jealous?"

Meredith laughed, too. "I don't know, but she's definitely eyeing you like she's miffed. Want to switch?"

"Sure." Jace stepped over to finish brushing Bella. "Hello, beautiful girl."

The horse nickered softly.

And Meredith gasped. "She actually wanted you to brush her. I wouldn't have believed it if I hadn't seen it with my own eyes."

Jace was floored, too. "It must be my natural charm."

"Yeah, Liza warned me about that," Meredith teased.

Jace slowed the brush to a stop. "What did she say?"

Meredith looked immediately repentant. "I'm sorry, I shouldn't have said that."

"But she did warn you." Jace wasn't surprised. Meredith's friend had warned him, too. Threatened him, more like, but still.

"Yes." Meredith stopped brushing Pete and looked over the horse's back at him. "She said that you've dated around a lot and to be careful."

"You've got nothing to fear from me, Meredith." He'd never disrespect her. She was the settling-down type and he'd never opened himself up enough to consider settling down.

Her eyes widened a little. "That's good to know."

He thought he saw a flash of disappointment in her gaze, but he could have been mistaken. Still, the silence that settled between them was deafening and Jace didn't like it one bit. Made him feel like an ogre. In a light tone, he asked, "After we're done here, can I see your spreadsheet of donations?"

"Of course."

Jace couldn't help but feel a little disappointed, too. Oh, he'd been teased about his reputation before, he'd even laughed it off several times, until he realized dating women for sport wasn't good for anyone.

Even if he considered going out with Meredith, he fell short. She deserved better. She deserved real and lasting. He didn't dare give in to this growing attraction he had for her. He didn't want to ruin anything for her business and he liked having her as a friend. Jace never could do serious, with all those expectations and deep feelings. The threat of loss hovered in the background, taunting him. Bottom line, he was a coward.

But if he could have a serious relationship that proved healthy, Meredith might be the one he'd consider.

Chapter Seven

Once inside her house, Meredith brought Jace into the dining room and opened the spreadsheet on her laptop. "There you go."

He bent closer to read it. "Wow, we've got some nice stuff here."

"And good price ranges, too, so there's something for everyone, affordability-wise, to bid on."

"A couple more big-ticket items might be nice."

"Like what?"

"I'll check with the car dealer outside of town. Maybe they've got a used car for sale they'd consider donating."

"Wow. That'd be—" *Over the top.*

Jace raised his hand to stop her. "Don't count on it, but I'll try."

Meredith nodded and stepped back so he could sit down as he perused her spreadsheet.

She hoped Jace hadn't taken offense to her comment about Liza. She couldn't believe she'd let it slip. He'd responded differently than she'd expected, too. Considering his confident swagger, she'd have thought he'd tease her back, or at least make a joke. Instead, he'd looked a little hurt. No, that was too strong a word, but he certainly didn't seem proud of his past. But then, he might have been surprised that she'd called him out on it, even if she'd been teasing.

Really, she needed to take his cues and back off. She had nothing to fear from him, he'd said. And that *had* kind of hurt. He had no interest in her as someone he might pursue for a date, which was good. She shouldn't *want* his interest or his attention. She couldn't afford to entertain such thoughts, but unfortunately, she did. Way too much.

Jace suddenly stood and walked to a door between the kitchen and dining room. "Where does this go?"

"To the basement."

"The hinges are crooked."

"I know. They've been that way since I moved in." It didn't bother her, really.

He turned to her. "I can fix that."

"It's fine."

He was already moving. "No, I'll fix it. It won't take long. I'll just grab my toolbox from the truck."

And there he went, helping her. Again. They teetered toward a very real friendship. Maybe that was okay with a volunteer, but Jace was going through his own therapy on Tommy Tuesdays. Even though she didn't guide his process, he still should be off-limits, yet she plowed forward as if she wore ethical blinders. It was a good thing she'd never told Liza about the specifics.

In moments, he was back inside with a cordless drill.

"Do you need help?" she asked.

"Nope, I got it."

Meredith glanced at the clock. It was getting late and she was hungry. Greedy for his company, and hoping to reciprocate with some sort of payback, she went out on a limb. "Would you like to stay for dinner? I'll fix something while you're fixing that. It's the least I can do."

"Sure."

"Cheeseburgers okay?" She'd never been bothered by eating alone before, but for some reason, tonight, she dreaded it.

"Better than okay."

Meredith watched him take the first set of hinges off the door. They were old brass and probably original to the house. What was a little off-centered door in an old house?

What was she doing?

Meredith ignored her better judgment as she washed her hands and got to work on the burgers.

She glanced at Jace. He worked quickly and with confidence. Her cat had ambled into the dining room, sat under the table and eyed Jace, too, watching his every move.

Meredith quit gawking and wiped down the dining room table, moving her laptop to the far end. She set out plates, silverware and glasses with ice to the sounds of Jace fixing the door. It made her hyperaware of his presence. After grabbing a bag of potato chips and the jar of pickles she knew he liked, she placed them on the table.

By the time the burgers were done, Jace was, too. She poked her head into the dining room. The door now hung perfectly straight. "Looks good. Thank you." She was thanking him a lot, lately. "Would you like pop, iced tea or water to drink?"

"Whatever you're having is fine. Where's the bathroom?" Jace asked. "I have grease on my hands."

Meredith pointed toward the living room. "There's a powder room under the stairs."

"Hmm, nice place for it."

Staring at his hands that he brushed against the front of his shirt, Meredith diverted her attention back to the meal. She was plating the food when Jace reentered the kitchen.

"Anything I can help with?"

Once again, his presence took up the whole space and a bolt of awareness skittered through her. "Um, yeah, there's macaroni salad in the fridge if you'd like to grab that and meet me in the dining room."

"Okay."

Meredith watched him for a second or two, then hurried to the dining room. She sat down and looked up when Jace joined her. She felt overly warm.

His color seemed a little high, too, but then maybe it was only windburn from their ride. It felt like they were kids playing house, only they weren't kids and they weren't playing. Regardless of all the conflicts of interest, something felt right about this. Did he feel it, too?

Meredith blew out her breath. "Do you mind if I say a blessing over the food?"

He nodded. "I'd like that."

Meredith bowed her head. She couldn't shake how intimate this felt, sitting down to dinner and praying together. She'd kept her prayer short and simple, but added a silent plea. *God, please help me through this meal without doing or saying something I might regret.*

The next day, John slapped his back. "Want some lunch at the café?"

Jace flinched. His muscles were tender. "Yeah, sure."

"You alright?"

"Just sore from riding horses yesterday. We went quite a ways." Jace followed his older brother out of the downtown Rose River shop that they were in the process of gutting.

John had wanted both him and Jeremy on-site today to figure out what could be salvaged from demolition. "Jeremy, you coming?"

"Be right there." Their younger brother remained on the scaffolding, working on saving as much of the original tin ceiling tiles as possible. He was on the last row.

"How's the arena coming along?" John asked while they waited.

Jace filled him in.

"I'll try to swing by later this week."

"Swing where?" Jeremy came up behind them, ready to go.

"The riding arena," Jace clarified as they left the building and walked across the street to the Rose River Café.

"Ah, your horse lady." Jeremy gave him a cheeky grin. "You're over there after work quite a bit."

Jace tried to blow off that observation, but couldn't. "I enjoy working with her horses and we're friends."

Jeremy nodded. "Ah, is that what you're calling it now?"

Jace knew his younger brother was only joking, but the verbal poke was true. Jace didn't have friends who were women—a few enemies, perhaps. For the most part, he'd never gone beyond a few dates. In fact, he didn't have any close friends besides his two brothers. Jace pushed Jeremy's shoulder, teasing back. "Maybe, if I didn't hang out with you two all the time, I'd have some real friends."

"Nothing wrong with having a tight circle," John added.

"If my circle got any tighter, I'd be alone." Jace glanced at Jeremy and they both laughed. Being alone had never appealed, but now? Without his usual dating distractions, it was much worse.

Jeremy gave his shoulder a squeeze. Surprised by the rare show of affection, or maybe it was understanding, Jace reached out, but Jeremy followed the hostess to a table.

Jeremy surrounded himself with a lot of people—a group of tight friends he'd hung out with for years. On the outside, his little brother appeared light-hearted and without a care in world, but Jace knew better. The loss of their parents was still clamped around his little brother's heart like a vise. They all had remnants of unresolved grief that hung deep inside like eternal icicles.

Jace had never really examined how he or his brothers had grieved or not, until recently. He glanced at John as the three of them sat by a window overlooking the Rose River and were given menus. John was the most predictable of the three of them, or maybe the steadiest. Not given to trying anything unusual or different, John barely gave the menu a look. He set it aside, knowing what he wanted probably before they'd even walked in.

John cast his gaze toward him. "Just be careful with this woman until after the job is done."

"Of course."

As if Jace needed to be reminded. He'd never place Three Sons Construction in jeopardy for a client. No romance until after the job was complete and payment received. Although, he shouldn't entertain any ideas of romance with Meredith. He hoped to continue to volunteer even after the job was complete. He didn't want to endanger any of that with a soured relationship.

"Speaking of which," Jace began. "I'll be over there tonight and going forward on Tuesday evenings to volunteer with one of her sessions."

"What do you do?" Jeremy asked with genuine interest.

"I interact with one horse, while the kid works with the other. Sort of like moral support, since he's not used to horses and neither was I."

"Until now," John added.

"Yeah." Now, he loved every minute with those horses.

Jeremy shook his head. "I don't get it. What's a horse going to do for someone who's messed up?"

Jace thought about that a moment. For him, there was an undeniable connection that felt safe. "Horses are intuitive. A person can let down their guard and simply feel without rejection or judgment. I don't know, Meredith can explain it best, but the horse is where it all starts in getting folks to open up enough to let go of stuff."

John's eyes widened. "And it really works?"

Jace shrugged. "I don't know. All I know is that the look on that kid's face before he interacted with Pete, one of the horses, and then afterward, is something I'll never forget."

Both his brothers nodded, but the waitress came to take their order, bringing an end to the discussion. But Jace kept thinking about the way Bella reacted with him, as if sensing the pain he carried deep inside. He wondered if maybe that was why Jeremy repeatedly brought home strays. Did he attempt to assuage his loss by trying to save a creature in need?

Jace listened while his brother rattled off his usual order of a deluxe cheeseburger with fries. Was John's strong work ethic and protectiveness over the business's reputation his way of honoring their parents? Always the solid rock in their family of three, how had John come to terms with their loss so it no longer hindered him? Had he exorcised that pain or was he keeping it buried because he'd had him and Jeremy to look out for?

Jace carried a debt he could never repay his older brother. Not that John would ever expect him to. They were family. And family looked out for each other. But if Jace could come to terms with his fear of loss, maybe that would also set John free. And Jeremy, too. If he could somehow share what he'd learned through Meredith's equine therapy sessions with his brothers, maybe it'd help them all.

Tuesday evening was rainy. It had rained on and off all day and Meredith was more than grateful for the indoor arena. She planned to have Tommy's session inside even though the soft, sandy floor wasn't complete. They wouldn't be riding, so no harm done. And Jace had agreed to help her bring the horses inside early, so they could get used to the arena before Tommy showed up.

Meredith walked Pete into the vast space. His ears twitched this way and that as the horse looked around. Meredith glanced toward Jace leading Bella. "Just walk them around at first, so they can get used to the openness."

"Sure thing." Jace walked with her mare, cooing supportive sounds and words her way.

For such a tough construction guy, Jace had a sweetness to him that she couldn't help but like. Who wouldn't? And yet, as Liza had said, Jace had kept his distance from any serious or long-term relationships. That was a huge red flag. Was he truly unable or simply unwilling to connect on a deeper level? But then, she wasn't much different. She viewed men through the lenses of past hurts and her father's betrayal.

She glanced around the open arena. "What do you think, Pete? You like?"

The horse nickered, but kept a careful watch on the surroundings.

She and Jace had blocked off the openings for doors with tacked-up straps. The big, garage-door opening had been reinforced with stacked bales of hay, since the gate had not yet been attached. In spite of the dreary day, natural light streamed through the window and panel openings. It was exactly how she'd envisioned the space and more. The breezeway that connected the stable to the arena was wide enough for a couple of stalls on either side.

Just then, Bella danced back from a loose strap that blew around with a sudden gust of wind. More rain was on its way.

Meredith stepped forward to help, but Jace held on to the spooked horse, calming her instantly with a soft voice as he stroked her neck. "Nice job."

"I see what you mean about spooking."

"I think it's the Arabian in her, but once she's familiar with that strap moving around, she'll be fine."

"Good thing you brought them in before Tommy arrived."

"Of course." Meredith would never have not done so. Bella might be more flighty than Pete, but she was still a steady, gentle horse. The next turn around the arena, Bella pretty much ignored the flapping strap. And by the third turn, Jace secured it.

"Thank you." Meredith unhooked the lead rope from Pete's harness, so he could mosey around on his own.

Jace followed suit and unhooked Bella, too. But the mare stayed close to Jace, walking alongside him.

"You've got quite the admirer there," Meredith teased.

"The feeling's mutual." Jace scratched under Bella's chin. "So what's the plan for this evening's session?"

"I think we'll do the cone obstacle course. I'm hoping to use the course as a memory lane for Tommy, so he can work through those feelings of abandonment and share them with Pete."

"And will I walk my own course with Bella?" Jace asked.

Meredith nodded. "If you would."

"Sure thing." Jace shifted his stance, and nodded toward the picnic basket. "Can we break into those sandwiches now?"

"Of course." She walked toward the stacked hay bales, where she'd left their picnic dinner of sub sandwiches, chips and pop.

Sitting on a bale, Meredith watched the horses a second or two before opening the basket. Bella and Pete milled around the arena, checking things out and listening to the rainstorm blowing around outside.

"Man, it's coming down now." Jace sat beside her.

The sound of rain hitting the metal roof was loud, but the horses didn't seem to mind. "I'm so glad a ceiling will be installed with insulation."

Jace nodded. "It'll cut down on the noise."

She reached in the basket and handed a steak-and-cheese sub to Jace along with a bag of chips and can of pop. She'd texted him for his preference then picked up their dinner on the way home from work. "This was the perfect place for the garage door."

The opening for the huge door faced north into the pasture. Since the rainstorm came from the west, water wasn't coming in this side. The openings for windows on the west side were a different story, but the rain dampening the ground would dry.

"Thanks for this." Jace lifted his full-size sub sandwich.

"Of course. I appreciate your help with Tommy."

"Glad to do it," Jace said before taking a huge bite.

Bella ambled over with interest.

"Uh-oh, look who is coming to beg." Meredith laughed at the way her mare moved close to Jace, eyeing his sandwich. She reached into the basket and offered Jace a banana. "She might like this."

"Horses can have bananas?" Jace looked surprised. He took the fruit, peeled it and held it out for Bella.

She sniffed it before taking the whole thing.

"Pete loves them." As she said the words, the horse trotted over. And so their indoor picnic was crashed by the horses, but Meredith figured that would happen and had packed a couple of bananas just in case. She held the fruit out to Pete, who took a bite of it, peel and all, as gently as a lapdog.

Jace laughed as Pete curled up his lip and shook

his head. He wanted more. "I never would have believed it if I hadn't seen it."

Meredith gave Pete the rest of the banana, then waved her hand. "Okay, you two, shoo."

The horses backed up. Some.

"They're still watching us." Jace took another bite of his sandwich as he eyed the horses.

Meredith unwrapped her sub of Italian styled cold cuts loaded with banana peppers. "They'll move along."

"Did you grow up with horses?" Jace asked.

Meredith shook her head while she chewed. "No. We moved to a more rural area when I was twelve and our neighbor had horses."

"The owner of Bella?"

He remembered. "Yes. His wife taught me to ride. She also introduced me to God."

"Nice. Were your parents cool with that?"

Meredith shifted. "Not at first, at least my mom wasn't. She was afraid I'd fall off the horse. But both my folks were concerned that I'd gotten involved in some cult when I started going to youth group at my neighbor's church."

Jace nodded. "Huh."

"Yeah, you'd think they would have been glad. It wasn't as if I was roaming the streets getting in trouble. Eventually, my parents didn't really care." Meredith picked at her sandwich. They'd stopped caring altogether, especially her father.

"And what about the horses?" Jace asked softly.

Meredith shook off her sorry thoughts. "Actually, I fell off of Bella the second time I rode her. I wasn't used to posting up, lost my balance and slid right off. Bella stopped, hung her head and looked at me as if saying 'what are you doing down there?'"

Jace chuckled.

"And that's when I fell head over heels, literally, for her and everything equine."

Jace's eyes darkened. "Have you ever been in love with ah, like, a guy?"

Meredith sat up straighter. "Ummm…"

He held up his hand. "Sorry, that was a little personal. You don't have to answer."

"No, it's okay. I thought I was once." She relaxed. A little. It was surprisingly easy to talk to Jace, but then, they were friends.

"Only once?" He tipped his head. "What happened?"

"He dumped me for my college roommate. She was blonde and beautiful." She looked Jace in the eyes, searching their depths. Was he the sort of guy who'd do the same thing given the chance? She wouldn't give him that chance. She couldn't.

"His loss," Jace said before looking away.

"What about you?" Meredith said, letting the question slip.

"What about me?"

Nice dodge. "Have you ever been in love?" She felt funny asking. They'd drifted into personal territory alright, but part of her really wanted to know what kind of woman Jace Moore would fall for. And part of her didn't, but she waited for the answer, anyway.

"Nope. Never." Jace balled up the wrapper of his sandwich along with the empty chip bag and stood. He pulled out a cell phone from his back pocket. "I forgot to return the electrician's call. I'll be right back."

Discussion was definitely over.

Meredith had hit a nerve. There was definitely more depth to Jace than he let on. He'd never *let* himself fall in love. No doubt that losing his parents like he did, and burying his grief instead of working through it, Jace Moore feared loss. Meredith understood that self-protective mechanism all too well. She had her own walls up most of the time.

What would it take to breach the walls Jace had erected? And even if she could, would she allow him to break through hers?

Chapter Eight

Jace stood with Bella in the middle of the arena while Meredith explained their obstacle course of colored cones. He and Tommy were to walk their respective horses through a winding trail of cones. This time, Tommy's mom had dropped him off and didn't try to stay.

He glanced at Tommy, holding Pete's lead rope. The kid was listening closely to directions. He wanted this. Whatever *this* was. Jace's thoughts kept wandering to Meredith. He didn't know why he'd asked about her love life. To know that some guy had broken her heart bothered him. Meredith was a kind woman. Grounded and real. He imagined that she'd felt the sting of rejection deeply. It was no wonder Liza had warned her away from him. He'd pretty much done the same thing.

Don't mess with Meredith.

Even John had warned him to keep a professional distance until after the arena project was done and paid for. He shouldn't blur the line between her being a client and more than a friend, but he couldn't help but wonder about the possibility of *more*.

He liked Meredith, but not getting too close was safer for both of them. He stroked Bella's neck as they swerved in and around the cones that had been stretched out the length of the arena to represent the twists and turns of life.

Jace walked slowly around his cones, so he remained behind Tommy, who was leading Pete. He glanced out of the large opening that had been blocked with hay bales. The rain had stopped and damp mist rose from the ground.

He couldn't remember enjoying an impromptu picnic of sub sandwiches more. With the rain pouring outside, he'd felt cocooned from the outside world. It had been intimate in a very mundane sort of way. That was something new to him. They'd chatted easily enough until it got personal. Also a new twist.

He concentrated on the current task, but glanced toward Tommy. The kid walked with stiff shoulders and a ramrod-straight back as if forcing himself not to feel. As if willing his emotions not to take him places he didn't want to go. Jace could relate all too well. Deep feelings opened up bad memories, like that night in mid-December—the night his parents were killed.

Why'd he think about that?

But the memory flashed before his mind's eye like the old photos and movies his parents used to play on a projector in the backyard on summer nights when they were little.

Jace watched that December night unfold in his thoughts as if he couldn't stop it—the paleness of John's face after he'd hung up from a phone call with the county sheriff. John had asked Jeremy to come down from his room. He'd gathered them both in the living room, near the Christmas tree his mom had so lovingly decorated with ornaments they'd all made for her over the years.

His heart tore open all over again. The pain from the worst memory of his life sliced through him with searing heat. So hot, he broke out in a sweat.

Jace stopped walking.

Bella did, too.

The horse stepped close and put her head down, against his.

He didn't know how long he stood there, his forehead against Bella's.

Tommy's voice intruded. "Hey, Mr. Moore. You okay?"

He looked at the kid who reminded him too much of himself. "It's okay to feel, Tommy. Really it is. You can't change what happened, but you can change how you deal with it."

The kid's face crumbled. "But it's not fair!"

"I know." Jace stepped forward.

Bella did, too. And Pete was nuzzling Tommy's shoulder.

And then, Meredith was close to the kid. "Tommy, do you want to talk to us? Or just Pete?"

Tommy wiped his face with his sleeve and looked right at Jace with runny, red eyes. "Did your dad leave you, too?"

It felt like a sucker punch in the midsection, so Jace glanced at Meredith for direction.

She gave him an encouraging nod, and pride shone from her eyes.

She was proud of him. Huh.

What he said or didn't say was up to him. Meredith had given him full discretion as if she *trusted* him. That was another first.

He took a deep breath and let it back out slowly. "In a way, yes. I lost both my mom and dad to a snowmobile accident when I was about your age. I have an older brother who stepped in to take care of me and my younger brother. My younger brother lashed out in anger, causing a lot of stress. I stuffed my grief, trying to make things smooth at home. I wanted to keep the peace and some sense of normal."

The kid's brown eyes widened. But he nodded for him to go on. Tommy understood.

"I never really unpacked that grief. Just let it lay there inside, tucked neatly away. I don't do messy. I keep everything tidy, so I…"

Tell the kid why you won't let anyone close. Maybe then Tommy won't make the same mistakes or worse. But the words stuck in Jace's throat.

"My mom thinks it's her fault, but it's mine. My dad doesn't want me around, so he left," Tommy choked out.

Jace reached out and squeezed the kid's shoulder. "It's not your fault, Tommy."

"He's right," Meredith interjected. "Whatever your father is dealing with, it's not because of anything you've done."

Tommy looked hopeful, but Jace could tell he didn't believe them. And if this dad of his was a deadbeat, then Tommy needed to come to terms with that, too. He'd need to deal with his feelings and not be afraid that others would leave him too. *Easier said than done.*

"Whatever the reason, Tommy, don't let it shut you down. Feel the loss but don't be afraid of connecting with others. Not everyone's out to hurt you. And more importantly, you can bring all this to God. He's an eternal Father who will never let you down or leave you." Jace couldn't believe those words had come out of his mouth. Words he'd never heeded, much less believed before. Until now.

He'd become friends with Meredith. Made a connection he'd never thought he could with anyone other than his brothers, much less a woman. Jace stroked the mare's neck, before looking at Tommy. "And there's Pete. He's going to sense how you're feeling. You can be real with Pete."

Tommy smiled then. "Like you with Bella?"

"Exactly like me with Bella."

"You're okay, Mr. Moore."

This time, Jace smiled, feeling lighter than he could ever remember. "I think I will be. And you will be, too."

Jace glanced at Meredith.

She stepped forward. "Well, Tommy, before your mom comes to pick you up, let's lead the horses back to their stalls for a bit of grain."

"Sounds good, Miss Meredith." Tommy turned to lead Pete back to the stable.

Jace did, too, but Meredith stalled him with a light touch to his arm.

"Thank you." She squeezed and let go. "I'll take Bella so Tommy and I can debrief."

"Sure, okay." Jace watched her walk away.

He prayed that the kid would open up more to Meredith now that he'd finally let down his guard. And Jace had a feeling that maybe he would, too. Tommy Tuesdays were as therapeutic for him as they were for the kid. Jace had never verbalized his own fear of connection before. Not until Meredith. This was the second time, but now, he could see it all so clearly. He was afraid to let himself fall in love because he couldn't handle losing another loved one.

Something to work on for sure. Going forward.

He glanced toward the stable entrance, hearing the murmurs of Meredith and Tommy talking. He replayed parts of their dinner conversation—Meredith had been hurt, too. And she'd mentioned a rough time in her teens when they'd first met. Had she worked through all that? He wanted to know. In fact, he wanted to know a lot more about Meredith Lewis. Other than admitting her college heartache, Meredith didn't talk much about herself. Was that because of self-protective walls or her own strict ethical reasons not to share too much with him?

God works in mysterious ways.

He'd heard that his whole life, either from his dad long ago, or from the pulpit when he'd bothered to listen. But now, Jace saw that the Lord may have brought this project to Three Sons Construction to save Jace from himself.

After processing Tommy's session privately, his mom had come to pick up her son. Meredith watched as they backed out of the driveway, then returned to the stable, where Jace was brushing Bella. "Thanks for sharing that with Tommy."

He didn't look up from the long strokes he made over Bella's back with the curry comb. "Did you let his mom know how it went tonight?"

"I did. Strange thing, though. While Tommy waited in the car, Sue sounded like she might be making it harder for Tommy's dad to see him. She's been messing up visitation. She's not being honest with her own child. Or me."

Jace looked up with fire in his eyes. "You're kidding me."

Sadly, she wasn't. "We're going to have a meeting in my counseling office later this week. Hopefully, that will help. I think she's afraid that if she lets Tommy see his dad, she'll lose him or he'll choose his father over her."

Jace shook his head. "Why do parents put their kids in the middle?"

Because of divorce, lies and trying to protect in all the wrong ways? Thinking about the dysfunction in her own family, Meredith shrugged. "Fear takes a lot of shapes." Shifting gears, she focused on Jace. He'd had a breakthrough as well. "Were you close with your mom and dad?"

Jace resumed brushing Bella. The lines around his mouth creased deeper as he tightened his jaw. He didn't like talking about it, which made his reaching out to Tommy that much more compassionate. "We were a tight family. Still are, I guess. John keeps us together."

But not whole. Jace had admitted to being afraid of getting close to people. And that made sense, considering he'd tried to keep things smooth at home between brothers after such a horrific loss. Jace kept his interactions with others neat and tidy—nothing messy, like falling in love.

Meredith went out on a limb. "Have you given your loss to God?"

Jace set the curry comb on the edge of Bella's

stall. "I try to, but it's a hole that has always been there. Nothing seems to fill it."

Meredith winced at the defeated tone in his voice. She understood Jace's self-preservation, but what was with all the dates? He didn't do serious relationships—he didn't date long enough for that. So why go out at all? Why risk it?

But those were *her* reasons for not putting herself out there to get involved with a man. Not that she had many fellas asking her out, but she didn't exactly put out the welcome sign, either.

"Thank you for letting me be part of this," Jace finally said. "For taking a chance on me as a volunteer."

"You're welcome. You've helped tremendously. Tommy was drawn to you from the get-go, so there's that. I wouldn't be this far with him if it weren't for you." And Jace was working his own therapy with Bella, working through the hole that gnawed at him still. So this had been a win-win. Thankfully.

Jace gave Bella a loving pat and then exited her stall to stand in front of Meredith. "I forgot to tell you that the ice cream shop donated a hundred-dollar gift card for your silent auction."

"Really? That's a lot of ice cream. I might be tempted to bid on it myself." Meredith glanced out of the open stable door. The sun had set below a break in the clouds, leaving an orange glow in the damp, chilly evening. Maybe she'd leave the horses in their stalls tonight.

There were two ice cream shops in Rose River—an old-fashioned, sit-down parlor and a walk-up stand just outside of town, so Meredith asked, "Which place donated?"

"The one downtown. I popped over on a break."

The ice cream parlor. "Thank you. That's a great addition."

"I think so." Jace nodded. "What are you doing now?"

Meredith scrunched her nose. She had notes to make, and summaries of sessions at her day job to input. "The usual paperwork."

"I'd like to take you out for ice cream."

Meredith felt her eyes widen at the words *take you out*…

As they exited the stable, he said, "Maybe I should rephrase that. I'd like to treat you to ice cream, seeing as how you like it so much." Jace's cheeks actually reddened a little. "That is, if you'd like to go."

Meredith didn't turn down ice cream if she could help it, but going with Jace? Not wise. She gave herself a mental shake. She'd just been thinking how she kept men at a distance because of her own issues. Maybe she should go to prove that she could without the world ending. "Where?"

"Frosties."

The walk-up. They had the best chocolate malts.

Thinking about that, and throwing caution to the wind, she agreed. "Okay. Let me grab a sweatshirt."

He half smiled. "Good. I'll start the truck."

Meredith didn't waste time. She darted into the house and grabbed a sweatshirt, her purse and the red folder from the dining room table. After she climbed into Jace's truck, she lifted the folder in hand. "I brought the grand opening stuff with me, so we can finalize plans."

She might as well make this about work, so it didn't feel like a date. It wasn't a date. She wouldn't date Jace Moore. She couldn't. "The end of September will be here before we know it."

"It will, but I'm pushing to get the arena complete, since John needs my help with the reno downtown."

Meredith's heart took an unwelcome dive. Jace would be gone soon, back to his other projects. Back to his regular life. She'd gotten much too used to seeing him when she returned home from work. Used to him fixing small things around her house and working with Tommy.

Would he continue with Tommy Tuesdays throughout the fall? She hoped so. She valued his presence more than she'd thought possible. And she really appreciated his help with feeding the horses, riding and her grand opening as well.

On the drive to Frosties, Meredith caught a glimpse of her reflection in the huge side mirror and nearly groaned. The humidity caused her hair to frizz. Shorter strands had pulled loose from her braid and fuzzed around her face. She should have fixed herself up some, but this wasn't a date. This was merely friends and business owners whose paths had crossed for a while going for ice cream at a walk-up stand. No big deal.

So why did her heart race from merely sitting next to Jace in his truck?

By the end of the week, the arena was nearly done. Jace and his crew had insulated the roof and then installed the ceiling. The electrician had finished his work early, too, so Jace gave his small crew Friday afternoon off in order to enjoy a long Labor Day weekend. John planned to join him after lunch to inspect the work and then Jeremy would also be out, so the three of them could install the clear panels while the scaffolding was still in place.

Sitting on the opened tailgate of his truck, Jace took a bite of his peanut butter and banana sandwich. He and his brothers would be working through the weekend on the downtown shop renovation. John may have booked them too tight, but they'd make it work. The downtown project was big, but definitely good for business all around, so Jace wasn't complaining.

He'd finish Meredith's arena in plenty of time before her grand opening. They'd confirmed their original date of the third Saturday in September while eating ice cream. They'd looked up "Rose River community fall events" online and other than some hayrides, there were few conflicts listed. Jeremy's friend's band had agreed to play, so that was a go.

Jace was grateful that Meredith had brought her grand opening folder with her. Instead of revisiting what he'd revealed to Tommy, they'd discussed plans. Meredith promised to contact the local chamber of commerce, high school and radio station next week in order to advertise the event.

Spending time with a woman without feeling like he had to be *on* and charming was something new for him as well. He didn't have to be anyone other than himself—warts and all. He might not know much about Meredith away from her horses, but that comment she'd once made that horses were what got her through her teens lingered. What had happened to Meredith Lewis to instill the desire to run an equine therapy business?

He had to admit that opening up, even the little bit that he had, seemed to loosen the stronghold his parents' death had on him. Her counseling style must be more listening than telling. She didn't advise him or debrief the session like she did with Tommy. But that one question she'd asked made him think. For real. *Have I given the pain of losing my parents to God?*

He'd rolled that question around in his mind, over and over again, and couldn't say that he had. Jace had held on to his loss like a lifeline. His folks were dead and they weren't coming back to him in this lifetime. He'd never considered what God might do if Jace truly turned over the pain. If he'd offered up that hurt, maybe it'd help. Maybe God would finally set him free.

Crunching a few potato chips, Jace let his gaze wander Meredith's property. The pretty little farmhouse with lace curtains on the windows reminded him of his mom. Meredith had the same down-to-earth, no-frills approach that his mom had had. Salt of the earth, Joan Moore might have called her.

Hearing his mom's voice in his mind twisted in a bittersweet way. It still made him smile, though. His mom would have liked Meredith. Of that, he had no doubt.

He spotted his brother's heavy-duty crew cab pull into the driveway and park.

John got out. "Jeremy will be here in a few. Are you done eating?"

Jace took the last bite of his sandwich and brushed the crumbs from his hands as he slid off the tailgate. He downed the rest of his water and tucked the empty bottle in his small cooler. "I am now. Let me show you around."

Walking into the stable, Jace led his brother through the breezeway into the arena. The sun shone through the window and door openings as well as the cutouts for the clear panels above.

"Nice natural light in here." His brother looked around.

"That was the goal."

John continued to nose about, inspecting the electrical wiring. "The outlets seem a little high."

"A kick wall will be installed around the bottom of the arena. A safety measure to keep horses from getting too close to the wall when riding."

"Speaking of horses." John pointed at the large, garage-style opening that now had a real gate keeping the entrance closed off to the pasture. But both Pete and Bella poked their heads over the gate to see what was going on.

Jace chuckled and motioned for his brother to come close. "Meet Pete, the big blond fellow. And this. This is Bella." Jace stroked her neck.

John reached for Pete and the horse nuzzled his brother's hand. "They're friendly."

"They are." Jace continued to scratch behind Bella's ears.

John stroked Pete's neck. "You're a handsome fellow, aren't you, big guy?"

Pete's eyelids drooped at John's gentle ministrations.

"I can see why you like hanging out here. Did you know Mom had always wanted horses?"

That was news to Jace. "Why didn't they get some?"

John shrugged. "Dad never got around to building a barn. I think he would have, though, in time."

If they'd have lived.

"I could see Mom with horses," Jace said.

Maybe he'd inherited his affinity for the beasts from her. Of the three of them, Jace most resembled his mom, while John was the spitting image of their dad. Jeremy was a blend of the two, along with a lot of their wild, dark-Irish uncle Jack Moore "thrown in," as their aunt often said.

"She'd like what you're doing." John continued to stroke Pete's nose.

"With the arena?"

"No." John stopped petting Pete and faced him. "Helping with this woman's equine program. It's all over town that you're gathering donations for a silent auction for her. It sounds like a good cause."

"It's very good. It's even helping me. I mean, we've never really talked about how Mom and Dad's passing affected us. Even after all these years."

John looked thoughtful.

"Whoa, Jace. You did this? Nice job, buddy." Jeremy had entered the building. It was the first time he'd been here. He came to a stop before them and his grin faltered. "Okay, who died?"

John let out his breath. "We were just talking about Mom and Dad."

The blood seemed to leave their little brother's face, followed by redness around the ears. "Why?"

Jace stepped forward, spreading wide his hands. "We've never really talked about how it affects us and maybe we should. You know, like the three of us, together."

Jeremy shook his head. "No thanks. I'm fine. It's old news."

Impatience flickered across John's face. "They're our parents."

Jeremy's eyes narrowed. "They wouldn't want us beating ourselves up over it again and again."

Jace exchanged a look with his older brother.

Jeremy crossed his arms. "Look, if you two want to have some coming-to-Jesus moment, go ahead. I'm good. Now, can we get these panels hung? I've got plans later."

"Let's get to work." John closed the conversation.

And Jace let out a sigh. Was he the only one who wanted some healing here? Or had his brothers already been there, done that, without Jace knowing? He glanced at Jeremy, who approached the horses with his palms up, and shook his head. His little brother was more twisted inside than Jace would ever be. John, who knew? He'd always been responsible and solid, but he kept his feelings to himself as well.

"The dark one is Bella, the light one is Pete," Jace said.

Jeremy scratched under each horses' chin as if he was their best bud. His little brother had a way with animals and it appeared that Meredith's horses were not immune to Jeremy's touch. Both horses nuzzled up closer to his little brother.

Suddenly irritated, Jace said, "Shall we get to work?"

Jeremy grinned as if he hadn't a care in the world. "Now who's the impatient one?"

"Yeah, maybe I have plans later, too." He didn't. Other than hoping for a chance to ride with Meredith.

It was the Friday before a long weekend and Meredith probably had Labor Day weekend plans that didn't include him. Maybe he'd ask her. And maybe he wouldn't. He enjoyed being around her, and all things considered, the less time they hung out alone might be better. For now.

Chapter Nine

There were three pickup trucks with the Three Sons Construction logo on the doors parked near the arena when Meredith got home. She shut off the engine of her own pickup and got out. It had been a long week and she was more than ready for a three-day weekend. She hoped to work on making announcement posters for her grand opening event later tonight so they'd be ready to hang up around town tomorrow.

Walking toward the arena, she heard country music first, then voices. She stepped in through an open space that would be a door and didn't see anyone, until she looked up. There were Jace and his brothers. The men hadn't noticed her as they were up high on scaffolding, securing the clear panels just below the ceiling. She loved the natural light that poured in through those panels and it looked like the Moore brothers were finishing up the final section.

She stood below them, but her stable radio was

playing loud enough to make her shout. "Those look great."

Jace looked down at her and smiled. "We're almost done."

Meredith smiled in return, feeling butterflies take flight in her belly at the warmth in his gaze. Was he really glad to see her? She was glad to see him and that would never do. She liked him too much. At least the arena was close to completion. Jace would be on to another project, and hopefully her attraction to him would fizzle and fade.

She shouted again, "Anything I can do to help?"

He shook his head. "Nope. Thanks, though."

"I'll be right back." Meredith checked the time on her phone. It was only four forty-five, but they'd be done with those panels soon.

She rushed for the house and once inside, dumped her purse on the island in the kitchen. She foraged in the cupboard and whipped up a big pitcher of lemonade. Then she placed it on a tray with plastic cups filled with ice and headed back outside, toward the arena.

The guys were just climbing down the scaffolding when she walked in and set the tray on a construction table. Perfect timing. "I brought lemonade."

"I see that." Jace gave her that warm smile again, like they shared a secret. "Let me introduce you to my brothers. Meredith, this is John, and our little brother, Jeremy."

Meredith reached her hand out to each one. "Nice to meet you both."

John smiled. He seemed bigger than the other two, not so much taller, but more filled out. Obviously older, John had deep creases at the corners of his eyes, which were more blue than gray.

He took the cup from her. "Thank you for your business."

"Of course. The arena is turning out better than I imagined."

"That's what we like to hear," Jeremy chimed in as he also chose a cup of lemonade. "Thank you for this."

"Sure thing. It's a hot day today, but not bad in here. The ceiling insulation was worth it." She nodded toward Jace, who'd downed his drink and was refilling the cup.

Jeremy glanced from Jace back to her and then back to Jace.

What exactly did he see? Meredith remained quiet, praying there was nothing to see here—no attraction, no connection between her and Jace other than friends.

Jeremy gave her a nod. "My buddy with the band is looking forward to playing for your open house. I'll be meeting them later this evening. Any messages you'd like to relay?"

Meredith couldn't help but spot the mischief in his dark eyes. He had brooding good looks that seemed at odds with his relaxed, teasing manner.

"Nothing right now, but I would like his number so I can co-ordinate what they'll need to set up."

Jeremy pulled out his phone from his back pocket. "What's your number and I'll forward it to you. His name is Mitch."

Meredith rattled off her cell number while John and Jace walked around the inside of the arena, discussing what else needed to be completed before the final inspection.

"Jace speaks very highly of you and your program," Jeremy added. "He's the one who talked my friend into playing. Said it was a worthwhile donation."

Meredith glanced at Jace, feeling warmth spread through her. Hopefully, it didn't show on her face. She hadn't known the details, but hearing that it was Jace who'd pushed the band to play made her a little edgy. Was it simply a matter of good business advertisement for both of them, or dare she believe that Jace might truly care? He cared about the program and Tommy, that much she knew. There was no way this could be all about her.

She gave Jeremy her full attention. "Well, whoever talked them into it, I'm grateful. I listened to an online video and they're good. They will definitely draw people in, so tell your friends thank you."

She'd verify with Mitch that the band planned to play for free then find out how much they normally charged for an event and write them a donation receipt.

"I will. Thanks for the lemonade, I'm heading out." Jeremy set his empty cup on the tray. "See you guys later at home."

Both John and Jace raised their hands to wave goodbye, but kept talking, inspecting and basically going over the building.

Meredith remembered what Jace had said about his brothers being tight. They were family and the affection they had for each other was plain enough to see. She often wondered what it might have been like if she'd had siblings to talk to about the way her parents had split up and her part in it.

She'd had no one but Bella back then. Too embarrassed by the whole situation, Meredith hadn't even opened up to her school's counselor. Her mother refused to talk about the divorce, so there'd been no comfort there. Her father had given up all rights other than holiday visitations, and those holidays she'd stayed at his apartment, Meredith had felt in the way.

Meredith wasn't much different from Jace in that she'd buried the pain of her parents' divorce but not with the same motivations. She didn't want peace, she wanted absolution. She'd been so angry. When she hadn't been yelling at her parents, she'd been sulking and none of it had helped. Her tantrums had only served to drive a wedge between her and her parents. A wedge that remained to this day, especially with her father.

John and Jace walked toward her. Although there was a strong resemblance between them, she'd never have guessed they were brothers had she not known. They had dark hair in common, but Jace's features were more refined.

John spoke first. "I believe we'll be able to wrap this up for you next week."

"Great. Thank you for everything." Meredith's heart didn't match her positive voice. She'd miss Jace.

"Well, I'll be on my way, then. Nice to finally meet you, Meredith." John nodded and walked away.

Meredith stacked the empty lemonade cups, giving her something to do while Jace hung around.

"Got any big plans this weekend?" he asked.

"I'm going to Liza's family's camp between Rogers City and Cheboygan." Meredith shrugged, trying to sound casual. "What about you?"

"We'll be working on that downtown reno. What about your family?"

"My parents don't live nearby." Meredith gathered up the tray and headed for the house.

Jace followed. "Are you heading up there tonight?"

"No. I don't like to leave the horses too long."

"I can check on them for you."

Meredith stopped and turned. "I'd appreciate that."

"You can show me what to do tonight, if you have time. Maybe we can grab a bite to eat as well."

Meredith's heart beat faster. Surely, he wasn't asking her out. He was probably just hungry. Even so, she shouldn't be seen with him alone on a Friday night, as if they were on a date. "I think I can wrangle up something for dinner after we feed the horses."

Jace grinned. "Sounds like a plan."

They'd eaten together before, and this way, she could show him what to do for the horses while she was gone for a couple of days. No big deal. Right?

Jace washed his hands at the kitchen sink while Meredith changed her clothes upstairs. So much for his note-to-self of not hanging out alone with her, but he needed to know how to take care of Bella and Pete. He'd promised to swing by each evening to feed and check on the horses. He felt pretty confident in what to look for and Meredith would only be an hour away if anything came up. He heard a knock at the door before it opened.

"Hello? Merry? Oh, hello." A woman who was an older version of Meredith stood in the kitchen assessing him.

After drying his hands on a towel, he reached out. "Hi, I'm Jace. You must be Meredith's mom?"

The woman smiled and gave his hand a brief shake. "I am. Jerrilyn Lewis, nice to meet you, Jace. Where's Meredith?"

He heard her steps coming down the stairs. "Changing her clothes."

Meredith walked into the kitchen and her eyes went wide. "Mom! What are you doing here?"

"Did I come at a bad time?"

"No. Not at all." Meredith's voice didn't sound convincing. And why didn't she give her mother a hug?

"We were just going to make dinner," Jace added.

"Oh, no. I stopped to take you out to dinner. Both of you are welcome to go if you can." Her mom gave Meredith the once-over. "You might want to put something else on, dear."

Meredith had changed into a pair of long khaki shorts and a lightweight T-shirt of soft blue. She looked fine to him. Better than fine. Besides, there weren't many places in Rose River with a dress code.

"Every restaurant around here is pretty casual," he said.

"Oh. Then that's okay, I guess. I have to be on my way afterward to a friend's place up north, so we might want to take two cars."

Jace noticed that was news to Meredith. She

looked uncomfortable or disappointed, he couldn't guess which. Whatever she felt, Meredith quickly masked it. Something was definitely not right between the two women.

"You could have called," Meredith finally said. "We could have made solid plans."

Her mother looked away. "I wasn't sure if I was making the trip. Sort of a last-minute thing. So are we good to go out?"

Jace compared the two women who looked so much alike but seemed so different. Jerrilyn Lewis wore a lot of makeup, whereas her daughter barely wore any. Meredith's mom had shorter hair that looked overprocessed and dry, and her fingernails were bloodred. Her clothes were fancier, too, and expensive-looking. Sort of dressy casual.

"I'm game if you are." He glanced at Meredith, then at her mother. "Where were you driving from, Mrs. Lewis?" Jace figured it was someplace more urban than Rose River.

"Please, call me Jerrilyn. And I live outside of Lansing."

"Ah. College town."

"It is. In fact, I work in the communications department at State."

"Professor?" Jace asked.

"Social media manager."

"Ah." He didn't really know what else to say. He didn't know what a social media manager did, but knew it had to be more complicated than simply keeping a webpage updated.

Meredith had grabbed a light blue cotton sweater and draped it over her arm as she looked at him. "I should go. You're welcome to join us, as my mom said, but please don't feel obligated."

He couldn't tell by her lack of expression what Meredith wanted. He didn't have other plans, plus he was hungry so he didn't beat around the bush. "I can meet you at the Rose River Café or Charlie's."

The only two places in town that were open for dinner.

"Charlie's. The burgers there are the best," Meredith said.

"A burger joint?" Her mother looked skeptical.

"They have a wide selection." It was definitely the more expensive of the two, with steak and seafood on the menu, but that didn't really matter. Jace wasn't strapped for cash.

Meredith's mom smiled. "Then let's go."

"Alright." Meredith turned the lock then slipped past him as he held the door open for both women.

He caught sight of the cat sitting under the dining room table, and it made him smile.

Meredith's mom thought the smile was for her benefit. "Thank you, Jace, I'm glad you're coming, so I can get to know you a bit."

Jerrilyn must think he was Meredith's boyfriend. Jace's smile slipped a little. Obviously,

Meredith and her mom didn't talk much or she'd know he was her daughter's builder. And also a friend who happened to volunteer on Tommy Tuesdays. Jace shut the door with a light slam, and hoped tonight's dinner might shed some light about Meredith and her family.

Shifting gears, Jace decided to tell Meredith's mom exactly what they'd been up to. "Jerrilyn, would you like to see the new indoor arena for Meredith's equine program?"

"Oh?" Jerrilyn looked at Meredith. "Why yes. Let's take a quick look."

He caught Meredith's stormy gaze and couldn't tell whether the turmoil in those baby blues came from her mother seeing the building, or the fact that the woman didn't sound that excited about it. Jace may have fumbled the ball on that one. Maybe he should have left well enough alone.

"So is Jace your boyfriend?" her mom asked as they pulled out of the driveway.

Meredith chose to ride with her mom so they could catch up while Jace drove his truck. "No, Mom. Like I said, he's my builder and a friend."

"Does he own his own business?"

"With his two brothers, yes."

"Interesting. He seemed very at home in your kitchen."

Meredith didn't even respond to that.

"And he seemed to know a lot about your horses, too."

"He volunteers." That was the best way to describe it. The less details, the better.

Since she'd only ever had a handful of clients at most, her mother had never considered her equine program as viable. Although she'd said the arena was a very nice building, Meredith could tell her mother wasn't impressed. And she hadn't thought counseling was the right field for her all those years ago, when Meredith had chosen it for her major, along with equine studies. Not enough *stability*, her mom had said, which Meredith knew meant money.

"Maybe it's just as well."

"What is?"

"He's too good-looking. Like your father."

Meredith felt her spine stiffen. She didn't want to be reminded of that.

"Sorry that I rushed us out of your arena, but I don't want to be driving too long in the dark."

"No problem." Meredith shifted in her seat. "Where are you headed?"

"Presque Isle. A coworker invited me up for the weekend."

"That was nice of…them." Meredith wasn't sure if said coworker was male or female, and her mother wasn't offering any details. "Oh, take a right."

"Yes. I'm following your *friend*."

Meredith didn't miss the emphasis on *friend*, as if her mother didn't quite believe Jace was only that, or couldn't believe he was more. Like her mother had said, Jace *was* too handsome for her. Something she'd known from the start. Maybe it was a good thing that her mother had come and interrupted their dinner plans.

"Thanks for stopping," Meredith said.

Her mother smiled. "Of course. You were pretty much on the way."

"Yes." If she hadn't been, would her mother have gone out of her way to see her? They'd had an uncomfortable mother-daughter relationship ever since the divorce.

Neither one of her parents had asked her to spend the long weekend with them. And she didn't have a big extended family like her friend Liza. There were no summer cabins where everyone congregated for holidays. Not even a family reunion that she could remember. Only her grandmother on her father's side and she had passed before her parents divorced. That lonely feeling she'd often experienced as a kid resurfaced, making her shiver.

"Cold? I can turn down the air-conditioning," her mother offered.

Meredith slipped into the cardigan sweater, but knew the warmth she needed wasn't only physical. She longed to be cherished, cared for in a way that made her feel special. Valued. Wanted. "I'm okay."

Ha! That was a good one.

Meredith knew she wasn't. She protected her heart and soul with the best of them. She glanced out the window at the vast rows of maturing field corn with rolling hills just beyond. Rose River was a generous place, proven by the donations given for her silent auction. Whether those had come in because of Jace didn't matter. The people of this town cared. She'd find out just how much at her grand opening. Should she tell her mom about the event? Would she even come?

Her mother pulled into the parking lot of the restaurant and shut off the engine. "Well, this looks like a nice place."

"It is." Why was she so tongue-tied around her own mother? She got out of the car and followed her mom, who followed Jace into the restaurant.

It was busy, but the wait was only a few minutes before they were shown to a table tucked in the corner with a window view of a golden hay field that had been cut midsummer. Meredith inhaled the delicious aroma of steak and wondered if only a burger would satisfy. She glanced at Jace.

He accepted a menu from a cute waitress who'd come over to their table. "Thank you."

The waitress smiled back a little too broadly. "How are you, Jace? I haven't seen you in a while."

"I'm well, Cindy, and you?"

"Can't complain and even if I did, who'd listen?" The cute waitress laughed at her own tired joke before announcing the specials of a full rack of barbeque ribs and an eight-ounce sirloin steak. She promised to give them a minute to decide.

Meredith nearly rolled her eyes. Had he gone out with her, too? She glanced at her mom, who gave her an I-told-you-so look before studying the menu.

"So, Jace, do you live in the area?" her mom began.

"With my brothers, yes." Jace waved at someone across the room.

A guy.

But it didn't take long for another woman to stop by their table. "Hi, Jace. Taking two ladies out at a time now, I see. Sisters?"

Meredith watched her mom soak in that compliment with a big smile.

"Hey, Leah." Jace turned to them. "Jerrilyn, Meredith, this is our interior designer. Meredith has the indoor arena we're doing and this is her mom."

Leah gave her a big smile. "Nice to meet you both. And, Meredith, I have to hand it to you for wrestling a day's worth of labor out of these guys for your silent auction. That takes some skill. I can hardly get them to budge on estimates."

"John sticks with his original quotes," Jace insisted.

"Yeah, I know. So by the time they get to my costs, something always gets nixed." Leah looked over at the bar. "I gotta go. My friends are here. 'Bye."

"See ya." Jace didn't even watch her depart.

But Meredith did. She watched Leah meet up with another woman and two men. A double date perhaps? Didn't matter—she couldn't shake the sting of envy for Leah's polished good looks. Not a hair out of place on that one.

"You know a lot of people," her mom said.

"I grew up here."

"And what was that about a silent auction?" Her mom looked at her.

Before Meredith could answer, the waitress returned for their orders. Feeling irritable in addition to being hungry made her ravenous. Meredith ordered the sirloin steak special with two sides. A burger and fries simply wouldn't do tonight. She had a feeling nothing really would.

Chapter Ten

Jace poised his fork over his plate while Meredith attacked her steak with a vengeance. Why hadn't she told her mom about the grand opening? Meredith had been very matter-of-fact in her update, so Jace had filled in here and there, explaining that his involvement in the event was good for his business, too.

Meredith knew practically everything about his family and he knew so little about hers. Glancing at her mom, Jace cleared his throat. Not one word had been spoken about Meredith's father, so he took a risk and asked, "Do you and Meredith's dad live in Lansing or outside of it?"

Jerrilyn looked at her daughter, then focused back on him. The woman's warm gaze had gone cold. "Meredith's father and I have been divorced since she was thirteen."

"I'm sorry. I didn't know." He felt his neck grow hot. No siblings. Only Bella. That's all he'd known.

He glanced at Meredith, but she was still busy

with that steak, cutting it into small pieces. She could have told him, but then maybe he should have guessed considering her comment about Bella getting her through her teens.

Jerrilyn kept going. "I'm surprised Meredith didn't tell you that her father left me for someone else. But that's all water under the bridge."

He watched the woman dig into her Cobb salad. He wasn't fond of Jerrilyn's hard edges and lack of interest in her daughter's life. He turned toward Meredith, trying to convey that he was sorry for bringing it up, but she wouldn't look at him. Her parents were all she had, yet she obviously wasn't close to them. Why? He'd ask more later, but for now, he needed to lift this party of three up a little.

He turned his attention back to Jerrilyn and asked, "What do you do for fun in Lansing?"

She chuckled, obviously seeing through his attempt to lighten the mood. "I play pickleball. The college has several leagues. Have you ever played?"

Jace shook his head. "Nope, never."

"Too bad."

"I enjoy riding horses, though. Your daughter taught me and she's a great teacher." Jace didn't know where this need to prove how wonderful Meredith was to her own mother came from, but he let it stand. So what if he sounded like her boyfriend? Something felt right about it. Still, the thought of being with Meredith on a serious level, a commitment sort of level, had him shaking in his work boots. Could he get there eventually? Not until after the arena was complete and paid for.

"Which horse do you ride? Bella or Pete?" her mom asked.

"Both." He and Meredith answered at the same time.

He glanced at Meredith, feeling an incredible urge to grab her hand and give it an encouraging squeeze. But he didn't. He didn't think Meredith would welcome the gesture in front of her mom. And then, there was her concern about conflicts of interest, so he kept his hands to himself.

"Bella's been with Merry a long time." Jerri-lyn's blue eyes softened.

"She's helped me through a lot." Meredith looked at her mom with a bittersweet expression.

Was it memories of how Bella had gotten her through her teens, or the nickname her mother used that had Meredith looking so melancholy? It didn't really matter. That look tore at Jace. He wanted to draw Meredith into his arms and tell her everything was going to be okay. But sometimes, life didn't work like that.

"Of course," her mother merely whispered and looked away.

Again, Jace felt the mood at the table plummet. He wished Leah would come back; she was always good for a laugh or two. Instead, he finished his meal and the table fell silent.

Meredith picked at her plate and asked for a to-go container when Cindy returned to see if they'd like to order dessert. Jace would have, but both women declined.

He looked at the waitress he'd gone out with a few times. "I guess that's a no. I'll take the check."

"You most certainly will not," Meredith's mom interjected.

Jace just grinned. Despite his dislike for the woman, he wanted to make a good impression. Just in case something more developed between him and her daughter. "You can get it next time."

Jerrilyn smiled. "Well, thank you and I most certainly will."

Cindy returned with the container and check, and Jace handed over his credit card.

"Well, I should be heading out." Meredith's mom stood and extended her hand. "Thank you again, Jace, for dinner. It was nice meeting you." Then she turned to Meredith. "It was good seeing you, Merry."

"You, too, Mom." Meredith stood, leaned forward and gave her mother the smallest of hugs.

Jerrilyn returned the hug in similarly awkward fashion and then left.

"Wow," Jace whispered under his breath.

"What?"

"Nothing. She's not what I expected your mom to be like."

"She's…umm—"

"Bitter?"

Meredith's eyes clouded over with a mix of sadness, regret and remorse. "That's probably a good summation."

He jotted down a tip and signed the bill, taking a copy with him. With his hand at the small of Meredith's back, he led her through the crowded restaurant and to his truck.

She paused before getting in, her to-go bag swinging from her hand. "Thank you for dinner, Jace. Sorry it was awkward."

"No big deal." Once she climbed in, he shut the door, then slid behind the wheel, started the engine and pulled onto the road. "I'm sorry I brought up your father."

"You didn't know." Meredith nodded. "It's a sore subject, even now, after all these years."

"I see that."

The drive back to Meredith's house was a quiet one, but for the droning sound from their opened windows. His was all the way down, while Meredith's was only opened a crack. In spite of the warm evening temperature, she still wore the cotton sweater. She kept staring out the window and he felt like he'd failed her somehow.

Finally, as he pulled into her driveway, he asked, "Do you like being called Merry?"

"Huh? Oh, I don't mind it. It was my nickname as a kid."

"Tell me about that." He put the truck in Park.

"About what?"

"When you were a kid. Before things fell apart, were you close to your parents?"

"That's a tough one. I was closer to my mom, sure."

He shut off the engine. "What happened?"

"They divorced. Life changed."

"So you don't talk to them much?"

Meredith shook her head. "Nope, not much."

"Why not? I'd give anything to talk to my folks one more time. To see their faces—" His throat grew tight, so he stopped talking.

"It's complicated."

"That's a shame." He turned to face her. "Look, Meredith, death's the ultimate complication. You should talk more to them before it's too late. Before you can't."

She closed her eyes for a brief moment and when she opened them, tears had welled up. "You're right, of course, but then they keep their distance, too."

Jace could have kicked himself for making her cry, so he reached for her hand, glad when she took it and squeezed. "I'm sorry."

"Yeah, me, too." One of those tears tripped and fell from her eye to run down her cheek.

Jace traced the wet stream with his finger. Meredith looked like a bundle of hurt and he wished with everything in him that he might wipe away the pain as easily as he could a tear. Cupping her cheek, he was again taken with the softness of her skin and an overwhelming desire to kiss her.

As if he could.

Glancing into her eyes, he expected more tears, but Meredith merely stared back. Was she curious, too?

He leaned closer, pulling her face toward his, vaguely aware of the distress that flashed in her baby blues before they shuttered closed. Enchanted by her golden eyelashes that fanned across the top of her cheeks, he gently kissed each one, marveling at the softness there, too.

But it wasn't nearly enough. "Can I kiss you, Merry?"

Her eyes opened wide. Was she afraid?

He was afraid, too.

"Okay," she whispered.

Meredith melted. Her arms and legs might as well have been sticks of butter left in the hot sun when Jace whispered her nickname. It sounded so much sweeter when he said it.

As he brushed her lips with his own, Meredith heard warning bells along with her mother's words: *He'll never stay. Jace is too handsome for you.*

But then, Jace gently nipped at her bottom lip, and Meredith's thoughts scattered. In this moment, she cared only about the man in front of her. She wanted his kiss, even if it was tentative at first. Maybe Jace wasn't so sure about kissing her. Maybe those warning bells were ringing in his head, too. As they should.

Just then, Jace grew more insistent. It was even more delicious as he deepened their kiss, taking his sweet time until she couldn't stand it anymore.

She'd regret kissing him afterward, but Meredith wanted this and got lost. So lost, she didn't even notice that the truck's console dug into her side until it really hurt. She shifted and Jace pulled away.

She was about to tug him back toward her for round two when she saw remorse wash over his face. Kicking herself as the idiot who willingly walked off that ethical tightrope, Meredith's hopes were dashed. She knew better. This was her fault.

"Meredith, I'm sorry. I shouldn't have done that." He sat back in his seat.

"Why?" It slipped out as a mere whisper, but she had to know.

"Why?" He ran his hands through his hair, making the front stick up.

"Yes, why are you sorry?" She braced herself for any number of excuses he might toss at her, all while her fingers itched to fix his hair.

His expression was a mix of panic and wonder. It made him look terribly vulnerable and oh, so very dear. "Look, I'm not ready for this."

And there it was. *The truth.* Kissing him had been unconscionable. He might never be ready—

or worse, like Liza had warned, he might not have it in him. Just like her father never had it in him to stay true to her mother.

Okay, so she regretted their kiss, but it really hurt to see how much Jace regretted kissing *her*. She'd messed up royally, but at least Jace had been honest. Feeling her heart drop through the floorboards, Meredith reached for the handle and popped open the door. "Don't sweat it, Jace, it was just a kiss."

He nodded, still looking adrift.

Meredith didn't wait for an answer. She shut the door and headed into her house. She threw her purse on the dining room table and let out her breath. This was not good. Not good at all.

She peeked out the window.

Jace was still there.

She could see him, staring straight ahead. Would he reconsider and come after her? Meredith's heart skipped a beat or two. Nope, he restarted his truck and backed out of her driveway.

Meredith closed her eyes and relived the sensation of Jace's mouth on hers. She'd never been kissed so thoroughly, so gently, or so well!

Obviously, he'd had lots of practice.

She slumped into a dining room chair. Her mother had been right. He was too good-looking for her. Too handsome to keep as her own. The fact that he not only volunteered for her program, but also had been participating on his own in Tommy's sessions made him off-limits, anyway, but for a moment, Meredith had hoped. And that was as ridiculous as it was dangerous. If Jace felt taken advantage of, he could complain to any counselor who'd listen and she might lose everything—her license, and her livelihood.

But Jace wouldn't tell. She knew that in the depth of her being. If anything, he'd stick up for her. Like he had with her own mother. Nope, Jace Moore would mosey on to someone new because that's how he rolled. At least, that's what Liza had said. Was that still true even after his breakthrough with Bella?

Her cat, Willem, jumped on the table and butted his head against her shoulder. He wasn't supposed to be up there, but Meredith didn't shoo him away. Instead, she scratched behind his ears.

The cat started to purr.

"What am I going to do?" She let out a deep sigh.

Kissing Jace Moore only made him more attractive. At least she had the weekend to get over it. The next time she'd see Jace was Tuesday. Plenty of time to get over the awkwardness of a misguided kiss. Meredith grabbed her phone and texted Liza.

If the invite is still open, I'd like to come up to your family's cabin.

Her phone dinged immediately with a reply from her friend.

Yay! So glad. There's plenty of room if you'd like to stay for the whole weekend.

Tempting, but Meredith had things to do tomorrow—grand opening posters to make, for one. She'd drive up Saturday afternoon and try her best to forget kissing Jace. The horses would be fine for a couple of days. She'd make sure they had enough extra hay, and would fill the pasture trough with fresh water before she left, just in case Jace forgot to check on them.

Meredith texted back about when she'd arrive and that she'd let Liza know when she left her house. She needed to get away, if only for a little while.

Her phone dinged again, and Liza replied with two thumbs-up emojis and several exclamation points, making Meredith smile. Should she tell Liza about the kiss? No.

Nobody can know.

Antsy, Meredith got up from the table and headed outside to check on Bella and Pete. Anything to keep her mind off that kiss. And Jace. Once in the stable, she opened the sliding door that led to the pasture and sure enough, both horses trotted toward her.

She petted each, glad that Bella lingered near her. "Oh, Bella, I'm in way too deep."

Bella seemed to nod.

And Meredith laughed.

She opened the stalls for her horses and then went about getting them each a small scoop of grain. They'd already been fed by her and Jace before her mother had shown up, so this was simply a treat. The sweet scent of molasses from the grain, as well as the sounds of her horses munching, calmed her somewhat, but her heart mocked her as a fool.

She didn't want to fall for Jace Moore. He was wrong for her in every way that mattered. That kiss was unwise, and like her mom had said, he was too handsome. Everywhere they'd gone together, women either noticed him or had dated him. She needed to remember that and never, ever kiss Jace Moore again.

Late the following evening, Meredith sat by the campfire staring into the flames. Only her and Liza remained; the rest of Liza's family had gone inside to escape the night's chill and were playing a rousing game of euchre. Meredith chuckled at the shouts and laughter coming from the big cabin.

Jace had texted her earlier, letting her know the horses were fine and even Willem looked fine from the dining room window. She'd thanked him, and let him know she'd be home Monday in time to feed the horses. Jace wasn't a bad guy—far from it. He had some issues connecting on a deeper level with people, women in particular, but even if he was ready to commit, would he ever do so with someone like her?

"Penny for your thoughts." Liza had skewered a couple of marshmallows onto a long fork and held it out over the fire, and was turning it this way and that.

Meredith watched the white puff turn brown.

"You look pretty deep in whatever you're thinking about."

Meredith shrugged. "Nothing much. Jace texted that the horses and my cat were fine."

"That was nice of him to check on your place." Liza carefully turned the fork to toast the marshmallows' other sides before glancing her way. "You like him."

Meredith wasn't sure how to answer that. Her feelings for Jace were stronger than she wanted to admit. She looked at her friend. "What really happened with you two?"

Liza pulled the fork away from the flames just in time. "Get the graham crackers and chocolate."

Meredith had two sets ready to go. She sandwiched one of the roasted marshmallows between crackers stacked with chocolate and handed it over to her friend. Then she repeated the action for a s'more of her own.

Liza set aside the roasting fork and took a big bite. "Mmm, good."

Meredith chuckled at her friend's muffled reply. "So? You never answered my question."

Liza grinned. She had melted marshmallow smeared on her upper lip. "Ah, but you never answered mine."

Meredith contemplated her s'more and squeezed the graham crackers together in an attempt to melt the chocolate. Marshmallow oozed over the sides, getting her fingers sticky. "I like him. Now, tell me what happened."

"Nothing *happened* and that was part of the problem. He'd started coming back to church and asked me out. We went out several times and I thought maybe we were on to something, but just when I asked about that, he ducked out of sight, never calling me back, but then you already know all that." Liza's voice was matter-of-fact. "Maybe you should come to my church. He goes there regularly now."

"Maybe." Meredith tried to remember what Liza had shared back then. All she really knew was that her friend had fallen for Jace and he'd disappointed her. He'd gotten cold feet and run. Did Meredith really want to know the nitty-gritty?

Yes, she did.

"So what was he like?"

Liza tipped her head. "What do you mean? You know him."

Meredith took a bite of her gooey s'more, thinking how to best explain what she was asking. "Oh, I don't know about that. He's my builder and he volunteers his time helping me with the grand opening and all, but I wondered if he acted differently on a date."

Going for ice cream, and dinner with her mom, could *not* be considered dates.

"He's smooth, that's for sure. He asked questions to get me talking, joked around and was basically charming, you know?"

Charm oozed out of Jace, but there had to be more. Maybe something she'd missed. "Charming how?"

"He held open doors, pulled out chairs, that sort of thing. He'd even unfolded my napkin at Charlie's, before he took his seat, but I never really got to know him, come to think of it. Our conversations revolved around me and my interests. He has this way of making you feel like you're the only woman in the world. I got caught up in that."

Meredith felt a kernel of hope pop within her. Jace had opened up with her, Tommy and even Bella. He'd been real. And just as suddenly as it popped, the little kernel shriveled up and died. Obviously, Jace didn't look at her as someone he'd date. He wasn't *smooth* with her. He'd kissed her, sure, but probably because he'd felt sorry for her after she'd practically cried in his truck. He'd regretted it and she did, too.

Jace was too much like a bowl of popcorn. Meredith loved the stuff, but one taste was never enough. She wanted more. A whole bowlful doused with butter and salt.

Gathering her courage, Meredith asked, "Did he kiss you?"

"Oh, no," Liza said with compassion shining from her dark eyes.

"What?"

"You're falling for him," Liza accused.

Meredith inhaled sharply. There was no way she'd lie to Liza, but she didn't have to give her the whole truth. "I'm not. I'm attracted to him, but that's just not a good idea. Not with so many obstacles."

"I don't know if he has it in him to get serious and settle down." Liza loaded up the roasting fork with a few more marshmallows. "To answer your question, yes, he sure did kiss me. Quite a few times. I'm not going to lie and say it wasn't wonderful, but I think he was just going through the motions. And that was disappointing."

Meredith laughed. "Why'd you go out with him?"

Liza shrugged. "I don't know. He'd always seemed like a bad-boy type who'd be fun to tame."

Meredith nodded. She'd never wanted a bad boy and didn't think Jace quite fit that description. He'd said that he wasn't ready for a relationship. He'd been honest in that respect.

Meredith finished her s'more and brushed her sticky fingers against her jeans. "You're too good a person not to find that right man. It's just a matter of time."

Liza laughed. "Funny, but Jace said something similar."

"See?" Meredith smiled.

"The same could be said for you, too. Your Prince Charming will come."

"I think I'll pass…for now, anyway." Meredith didn't need the emotional upheaval. This push-pull with Jace was bad enough.

Watching the flames, she snuggled deeper into her sweatshirt. The evening had cooled considerably. It was clear, and very still and quiet except for the outbursts coming from the cabin. The stars twinkled above and a sleek crescent moon hung in the sky, casting shimmers across the calm waters of Lake Huron. Summer was over. And Meredith suddenly felt sad.

Liza's gaze narrowed as she turned the roasting fork again. "Has he, like, come on to you?"

Meredith grimaced at how coarse that sounded. He'd kissed her, but it hadn't seemed like smooth moves. More accidental than anything and comforting. And so very nice, like time had stood still, but wrong on all levels.

"No," Meredith finally answered.

"Good. Oh, no!" Liza pulled the roasting fork back, but not quickly enough. The marshmallows had caught fire, burning up in colors of blue and orange, hopelessly charred.

"No worries, there's plenty more." Meredith

reached for a couple new marshmallows from the bag and handed them over.

She only hoped the blackened marshmallows weren't a sign of things to come. If she didn't get a handle on her feelings for Jace, she and her career could end up burned to a crisp.

Chapter Eleven

Tuesday, Jace spotted Meredith's truck pull into the driveway. She was a little later than usual, but that had given him and his crew ample time to finish installing the windows and doors. His crew had just left, and all that remained was to build the kick wall, which he wanted Meredith's input on before starting, and then the arena floor would be completed with a top layer of sand spread by the subcontracted company from downstate.

Meredith would no longer be a client then. Her account would be paid and he'd be free to ask her out legitimately. But should he? Would she even go, considering his involvement with Tommy Tuesdays? That's where things got dicey.

He'd been truthful when he'd said that he wasn't ready for a relationship. But if the old saying that absence made the heart grow fonder was indeed true, the quickening in his pulse at simply seeing her truck confirmed it. He'd missed her these past few days and that scared him. Maybe more than their kiss. Still, he walked toward her.

She spotted him, smiled and waved, her red braid gleaming in the sunshine.

He yelled out, "Come see the windows."

"Be right there." She pulled out a couple of those reusable, grocery-store totes from the back seat of her truck and headed inside. She'd gone food shopping. That's why she'd been late in getting home.

She usually fed him on Tommy Tuesdays and he hoped the kiss they'd shared didn't change that. He looked forward to sharing a meal with Meredith, who'd become a real friend. It didn't matter if they sat on a couple of hay bales or at her dining room table. They'd talk about the upcoming session, the horses or the arena, and Jace could be himself. But now—

He flexed his arms and stretched. What was taking her so long? He wanted to show her the installed windows and doors, but also, he wanted to *see* her. To apologize once again for kissing her because he'd taken advantage of her at a vulnerable moment.

She came out of her house and walked toward him. She had changed into her typical jeans and T-shirt, but none of that mattered. His heartbeat had picked up and it took everything in Jace not to pull her close again.

"Hey," he said.

"Hi. Thanks again for checking on the horses while I was away."

She'd gone to Liza's family's cabin. Had they discussed him? He imagined that Liza didn't have anything good to say and rightly so. "Glad to do it."

In no time, they were at the arena and Jace couldn't stand the silence any longer. "So what do you think of the windows?"

Meredith nodded. "The ones facing me look great."

"Wait 'til you see the doors, too. They really turned out nice." Jace picked up his pace, feeling like a kid on Christmas morning. He opened the regular-size door and bowed. "After you."

Meredith gave a nervous-sounding half laugh.

Great. She was nervous around him. Man, he'd really blown it with that kiss.

Jace walked to the center of the arena and looked around, trying to view everything the way Meredith might. All he saw was beauty and function—beautiful windows and a functional, large garage-door-like entrance to the pasture. "Well?"

Meredith smiled then. "It's perfect."

"It is, isn't it?" Jace couldn't help but puff out his chest a little as he walked toward the large electric door that rolled up with a push of a button. "Here's the switch to open it."

Meredith touched it and watched as the door went up.

Jace hit the button again to stop it midstream. "You can halt it at any time, and then hit it again to resume, hit it a third time to reverse course and go back down."

Both horses moseyed over from the pasture and stuck their heads in.

Jace stroked Bella's nose, then focused back on Meredith. It was now or never to clear the air between them. "I want to apologize again for Friday night."

"Don't." She waved her hand in dismissal. "It's no big deal. I know I'm not your type."

Wasn't she? Kissing her had felt like coming home, but he wanted to know why she'd think that. "And what's my type?"

Meredith laughed. "Not freckled freaks like me."

He didn't find the comment amusing at all. Meredith was a natural beauty. "This has nothing to do with your looks."

Her eyebrows shot up.

He was only digging himself deeper. "Meredith—"

"Jace, let's just forget it, okay? I shouldn't have kissed you. I value your friendship and don't want to lose it, all things considered. I'd like to stay friends. Can't we just leave it at that?"

Friends.

That made more sense. For both of them. She was at the edge of growing her business and worried about some ethical code she followed as a counselor. He was simply at *the edge*, looking over a precipice with no idea what might lie beyond or beneath. Friends was definitely the *safer* choice. It was also disappointing and, he realized, not nearly enough.

He let out a breath he didn't realize he'd been holding. "Sure. Friends."

She smiled. "Good. Now, if you're interested, I bought stuff to make tacos. I can whip that up quick before Tommy gets here if you'll help do some chopping."

"Chopping?" Jace drew a blank.

"Tomatoes, lettuce, onion."

"Oh, yeah, sure."

"Then let's get to the kitchen." Meredith shooed the horses back out to pasture and pulled the newly installed gate across the opening.

"What about feeding the horses?" He followed her out of the arena toward her house.

"I thought I'd have Tommy help with that tonight. I think I'd like to teach him to ride soon."

Like she'd taught him. "Why? I didn't think riding was part of your program."

"It's not normally, but can be. And it will help boost Tommy's confidence."

"You're probably right." Of course, she was— this was her profession. Once inside, he bent down when Willem came forward for a scratch behind the ears.

Meredith washed and then dried her hands. "Would you like something to drink?"

"I'll get it after I wash up." He headed for the powder room under the stairs.

He'd been here plenty of times but tonight it felt awkward. Tonight, she'd pushed him back into the *friends* category. A place he didn't want to be, but he was too much of a coward to speak against it. The fact that he'd told her he wasn't ready for more hung like a clothesline, blocking the path. Unless he ducked under it…

No. Meredith deserved better than his usual few dates that were surface level with meaningless interactions. They were well beyond that, anyway. He didn't know how to have a real relationship with a woman. A meaningful one—one that would last. But he'd like to learn. With Meredith.

Friends, huh?

Definitely the safer choice, and until he could figure out how and when to move forward, he'd better stick to Meredith's request. He didn't want to lose what they had. He didn't want to lose her as a friend, and that's what would happen if he pushed too soon and they soured. That loss wouldn't be good for him and he knew it would eat away at her. Meredith didn't need any more rejection in her life. One problem remained, though. Now that he'd kissed her, he wanted to do it again.

Sunday morning, while Meredith got ready to attend Liza's church, she peeked out the window at the arena as if making sure it was still there. It was all done—completed to perfection. When she'd pulled into her driveway after work on Friday, she'd noticed that Jace's truck and his crew were gone. The area had been cleared of any construction material and the grounds had even been tidied.

She had walked through the arena door and stood in the middle of the space gawking, then she'd thanked God for making it happen. For the grant, for finding Three Sons Construction—everything had come together. She'd texted Jace to thank him as well. He'd responded that the final inspection would be sometime this upcoming week, as well as the final bill for payment. Jace had come in on budget, another thing she was grateful for.

She hoped she saw Jace at Liza's church this morning. If the truth was told, seeing him was part of why she'd accepted her friend's invitation. She'd been the one to reaffirm they were simply friends, yet here she was missing him.

Looking in the mirror, she hemmed and hawed over changing her hair back to her usual one or two braids. This morning she'd gathered it all up into a fat bun and the look was a bit severe. She pulled tendrils of red hair around her face to soften it. She also applied rose-colored blush and brown mascara, finishing up with a swipe of lip gloss. Checking the clock in the bathroom, Meredith didn't have time to change her hair or any-thing else. She had to go.

After rushing down the stairs, Meredith grabbed a jacket and stepped outside into a cool and cloudy September day. She hoped to ask Jace more about the final inspection—if she needed to be pres-ent. She'd also like to bring him up to speed on her grand opening plans. She'd already emailed press releases to the local newspaper and radio station. There was no turning back now. Not that she wanted to, but every time she thought about what was coming, a ripple of nerves settled in her stomach. Could she really pull this off? Could she grow RR Equine Therapy after all this or would it remain a dream instead of a reality?

Meredith climbed into her truck, started the engine and backed out onto the road. She knew the way and it didn't take long before she pulled into the parking lot of a church that looked more like a residence. She got out and spotted a famil-iar vehicle that had just pulled in. A bigger truck than Jace usually drove but with the same Three Sons Construction logo.

She waved.

Jace spotted her with a look of surprise.

She waited on the sidewalk as he came toward her, drinking in the sight of him wearing khakis and a blue button-down shirt and windbreaker. He cleaned up really well and her mom's words that he was too handsome echoed through her thoughts once again.

"What brings you here?" Jace asked.

"Liza invited me."

"Nice." His smile froze slightly, but maybe she'd imagined that. "Mind if I sit with you?"

"Not at all. I was hoping to talk to you about the upcoming inspection."

"You could have called." He nodded toward his brothers as he opened the door for them all to enter.

"I would have, but figured I might see you here." Truthful words. She'd stalled calling him, worried that if she had, she'd have no excuse to be here.

"You look nice," Jace said as she passed by.

Meredith felt her cheeks flush. She'd worn a simple pair of gray trousers with a matching turtle-neck sweater, but his compliment wrapped around her like a warm blanket. "Thanks, you do, too."

"Morning, Miss Lewis." Jace's younger brother gave her a playful wink.

Meredith laughed. "Morning, Jeremy."

John gave her a smile, too, yet both brothers kept walking and slipped through a set of double doors that were opened wide. A couple of kids squealed as they ran by her into the sanctuary. This place was louder and more relaxed than where she went and the people were mostly younger, too.

Meredith's breath caught when she felt Jace's hand slip to the small of her back, guiding her through those opened double doors. She spotted Jace's brothers seated toward the back and then saw Liza closer to the front. She waved.

Her friend waved back and held up two fingers. *Two seats.*

Meredith rushed forward, away from the warmth of Jace's hand, and gave her friend a quick hug. "Morning."

"Morning." Liza glanced at Jace. "Hello."

"How are you, Liza?"

"Good. I hope these seats are okay."

"I dunno. I might have to pay attention this close to the front," Jace teased.

"They're fine." Meredith turned toward Jace as she sat down next to Liza. There was no way she was moving. "Unless you'd rather sit with your brothers."

"Nope." Jace sat on Meredith's other side.

Liza squeezed her hand.

Did Liza know how awkward Meredith felt sitting between her and Jace? Really, she needed to shake it off already. Like Liza had said, there hadn't been much between them other than a few dates and kisses, even though her friend had hoped for more. What woman wouldn't have wanted more?

Maybe I want more too.

The music started, and then they were on their

feet again when the worship singers asked everyone to rise and join in a song, with the words on a screen near the stage.

"Thanks for coming," Liza whispered. "I know this is a little later than you're used to."

"Thanks for inviting me," Meredith whispered back.

She was an early riser and typically went to a more traditional church in town with a morning service that started at eight thirty, a full two hours earlier than this one. An early service was nice during the summer months as it gave her more time to enjoy the day and get chores done. Now that the mornings were cooler, sleeping a little later had its advantages, too.

Meredith sang several of the songs tentatively and with a quiet voice. She was used to a hymnal book. The voices around her were loud and clear. Everyone seemed to join in, but she noticed that Jace didn't sing at all. At least, she couldn't hear him, and he was standing right next to her.

Glancing his way, she noticed that his eyes were closed and his fingers tapped against his thigh to the musical beat. His obvious concentration touched something deep inside her. Like watching him connect with Bella, Meredith was seeing yet another side of Jace that she hadn't expected. He was communing with God, oblivious to those around him.

Her throat grew tight and her eyes stung. When

was the last time she'd gotten that lost in a song service? Had she ever? Meredith concentrated on the words being sung, but her mind continued to wander. She'd always been self-conscious and kept her feelings close, guarded. Maybe those insecurities had bled into the way she related to God.

It wasn't long before they sat down as the minister approached the podium to rattle off a few announcements. Meredith made a mental note to let the minister know about the upcoming grand opening event as well. Maybe he'd announce it in service the following week.

"How do you like it so far?" Liza whispered.

"I like it." In fact, she'd like to come back.

Meredith recognized a few folks, but didn't know many. The uneasiness of sitting between her friend and Jace had worn off, which was good considering that she'd like to return.

Glancing at Jace, Meredith couldn't tell what he might be thinking about the situation. Recalling how he'd said her looks had nothing to do with his type, she wondered what he'd meant. She'd been too afraid to ask him to clarify, afraid he didn't like what he saw when he looked at her, so she'd let him off the hook as much for her sake as his.

Shaking off those thoughts, she paid attention to the sermon and was struck by what the minister said. He stated that the deepest hurts were often caused by those who were closest and that could impact how a person viewed God and whether or not they'd trust in the Lord.

Was that her? Did she view God as an emotionally absent parent, making her rely on herself more than Him?

Jace's words about death being the ultimate complication came back to her. He'd been shocked that she didn't keep in touch with her folks. But then, she was the reason they'd divorced, something not one of them had ever forgotten. Perhaps as a person of faith, she should be the one reaching out to them, showing them the love of God, instead of waiting for them to make a move toward her.

Closing her eyes, she silently prayed for forgiveness and guidance. She counseled kids all the time to give their parents a second chance. It wouldn't hurt for her to extend that same grace to her mother and even her father.

She could at least try.

When the service ended, Jace leaned toward her. "Are you free for lunch?"

A shiver shot up her spine. It was just lunch. "I am. But first, I'd like to meet your minister and tell him about the grand opening."

"Come with me and I'll introduce you." Jace offered his hand.

Meredith hesitated.

"I won't bite, Merry." His voice was reminiscent of their kiss and his eyes challenged her as he waited with his hand extended.

No way was she taking his hand. Not here, not now.

"I'm not so sure about that." She wrinkled up her nose and walked by him.

She heard him chuckle, but he kept his distance as they wove through the crowded sanctuary. People chose to stick around and chat rather than leave right away and Meredith didn't want anyone getting the wrong idea about her and Jace.

But Meredith glanced at her friend and Liza gave her a concerned smile. Liza saw way too much. Regardless of the appropriate, physical distance between Meredith and Jace, were her feelings for him plain to see?

Jace pulled out a chair for Meredith near a window in the Rose River Café. "How did you like church?"

"I liked it."

Meredith scooted her chair in on her own, so he sat opposite her. "Ever been there before?"

"Nope. Liza has been after me for a while to go." Meredith adjusted her napkin on her lap. She peeked up at him. "I might start going there."

"I'd like that." He'd like seeing her Sunday mornings. Now that the arena was finished, Tommy Tuesdays were the only excuse to go over there, and who knew how long the kid's sessions would continue.

"You would?" Confusion flashed in her pretty blue eyes.

Her lashes had been darkened with mascara, but he rather liked the natural golden color that was unique to Meredith. "I would."

"Why?"

Why indeed?

He'd opened himself up with that one. Working at her place, he'd looked forward to helping with the horses and Tommy Tuesdays. Those things were the best parts of his day, next to horseback riding with her. Somewhere along the line, Meredith had become his closest friend. Maybe his only friend, outside of his brothers. But he wanted more. And he'd like to give *more* a try.

"It's a good church," he finally said, chickening out.

Really lame.

"Oh."

Was that disappointment he heard in her voice? She'd been the one insistent that they remain friends. She rallied quickly, and added with enthusiasm, "That sermon made me think that I should invite my parents to the grand opening."

Shocked that she hadn't already, he asked, "What part of the sermon gave you that idea?"

She shrugged. "The part about forgiveness. Although, it won't be easy inviting both. My mother won't go anywhere near my father. She didn't attend my high school graduation because he was there."

Jace couldn't even imagine. "I'm sorry."

"It stinks, but maybe if my father comes early, my mom can come later or vice versa."

"When are you going to call them?"

"After I get home. I want to put up a few more announcements about the grand opening on community boards here in town, like at the grocery store, and the bakery, and here on our way out." She pulled an eight-by-ten flyer from her purse. "I printed these at work with the color printer in my office."

He took the flyer, loving that she sounded more excited than nervous. Looking over the brightly colored announcement, complete with a picture of her and the horses, along with the date and activities, Jace smiled. "This is good. It'll be here before you know it."

"You'll be there?" Wariness crept into her eyes.

"Of course, I'll be there. I'm your master of ceremonies, remember? I'll help you set everything up, too."

"Good." She finally looked over the café menu.

Jace reached across the table and covered Meredith's hand with his own. "It's going to be great."

"It will be." She pulled her hand back as the waitress arrived to take their orders. "I'll have a cheeseburger deluxe and fries and more water."

"Make that two," Jace told the waitress, in a hurry to see the woman leave. He thought about taking Meredith's hands in his again but she held them in her lap.

"So about this final inspection, do I need to be there?"

"No. John and I will meet the guy at your place. It should be pretty quick. John has already looked everything over, so I don't anticipate any issues."

"Your brother knows what they look for?"

Jace downed the rest of his water. "He does."

Meredith nodded. "I want you to know that what you said about wishing you could speak with your parents stayed with me. I need to reach out to mine more and at least try to fix what was broken."

Jace didn't hesitate to reach across the table again. He was glad when she placed her hands in his and squeezed. "That's good. If you need anything from me, you only have to ask."

She stared at their hands. "I'll let you know how it goes Tuesday night."

"Tommy Tuesdays."

Meredith smiled. "Yes. The big first ride. You're still planning to come?"

"Of course. I gotta see Tommy ride. He'll love it."

"He'll love that you're there for his first time."

Jace grinned. "That's what friends are for."

The waitress arrived with their food and Meredith pulled her hands away. Feeling bereft of her touch, he knew what he harbored for her was far from only friendship. It wasn't anything he'd ever felt before, either. Wanting to simply hold a woman's hand wasn't exactly his style. Rather, it hadn't been.

Meredith was different, and definitely not like the women he'd dated. Meredith was exactly his type—interesting and warm. Brave and smart and down-to-earth. She was all those things wrapped up with natural beauty that grew more attractive rather than less.

He wanted to move forward, but what if she wanted to remain simply friends? He didn't know which option worried him more. All he knew was that he didn't want to lose what they had. He didn't want to lose her. The mere thought of never seeing her again made his stomach knot. He needed to tell her all that and promise they could take it slow, because he wanted their relationship to last.

Regardless, he shouldn't do anything until after Meredith's grand opening event because he wouldn't jeopardize that day for anything. He owed it to her. And he owed his brothers the good PR it would provide Three Sons Construction.

Which meant a couple more weeks of only holding her hand.

Chapter Twelve

"Hi, Tommy." Meredith met her client in the driveway, so she could talk to his mom. "Why don't you go on down to the stable. Jace is there."

The boy nodded and took off at a run.

Meredith turned to his mother. "Hi, Sue. How are you doing?"

"Pretty good, actually. Tommy is so excited to ride Pete. It's all he's talked about for days."

Meredith was glad to hear that. "You're welcome to stay and watch tonight. The observation booth is complete."

Sue looked tempted but shook her head. "No. He prefers that I don't watch and I need to respect that. Maybe the next ride. I'll be back in an hour and a half, and next week his father will drop him off and pick him up."

"That sounds great, Sue. Thank you for the heads-up." Meredith was pleased to see Tommy's parents finally working together rather than against each other. It was a delicate balance to be sure, but already, Tommy's parents were doing better than her parents ever had back in the day.

Her mother and father had agreed to come to her grand opening event, in shifts, of course. Meredith had been pleasantly surprised that both seemed delighted that she'd asked them to attend. That was progress. Especially for her. She'd reached out first.

Meredith hurried into the stable after Tommy's mom drove away. The evening air had cooled, but the stable and the arena still held the afternoon's warmth. Jace and Tommy were chatting away when she walked in. They had Bella and Pete out of their stalls, hooked to lead ropes, ready to be saddled.

Meredith smiled. "Ready?"

"For ages," Jace teased.

Tommy chuckled.

"Okay, let's head for the tack room." Meredith led the way, loading Tommy up with the saddle and blanket first. She didn't include a harness, as they'd work on reins the following week.

She instructed Tommy how to get Pete ready to ride while Jace saddled up Bella. The kid did everything perfectly, but the closer they got to mounting up, the quieter the boy grew.

Jace donned a helmet and climbed onto Bella.

Tommy looked hesitant. Scared.

"You can do it, Tommy," Jace said.

Tommy looked up at Jace and went pale, as if

he was at some great height. Tommy stared at the saddle on Pete's back. "I don't know."

"What scares you?" Meredith finally asked.

Tommy looked at her. "I don't want to fall off."

Meredith handed Tommy a helmet. "I can't promise you won't, but I can promise that you'll never know unless you try."

"But I could get hurt." Tommy looked at her like she should know better. She was the adult, after all.

"That's why we wear helmets and start out slow." Meredith smiled gently. "Fear of getting hurt is a powerful motivation, Tommy. I won't argue with you there, but it can keep us from enjoying life to the fullest. It can also be wrangled into submission by being careful and weighing out the advantages of what you want to accomplish against the risk of injury."

He considered her argument.

"I'll walk you around the arena until you get the feel of the saddle and your balance. You can stop when you want, and we never have to do it again if you don't like it, but I encourage you to try."

She glanced at Jace, who had listened to her as well. He gave both her and Tommy an encouraging nod.

Tommy took the helmet from her hands with determination. Then he stroked Pete's nose and whispered to the horse, "Take care of me, okay?"

Meredith couldn't help but glance at Jace once

again, but he was deep in his own thoughts. Some-thing about this whole situation reminded her of him. And herself, too.

"Okay, I'm ready." Tommy had tightened the strap of his helmet.

"Good job saddling Pete." Meredith took hold of the horse's lead rope and walked the horse toward the mounting block she had pulled out earlier, in prep for tonight. "Okay, Tommy, I'm holding Pete, so you can climb up the block."

Tommy did as she asked, so Meredith continued her instructions. "Take hold of a chunk of Pete's mane with your left hand, and set your right hand, palm down, in the middle of the saddle. Place your left foot in the stirrup with your toes pointed toward Pete's nose."

Tommy did that, too.

"Now, stand up in the stirrup—yes, that's per-fect—and now swing your right leg over so you're sitting in the saddle."

Tommy hesitated a moment, looking scared when he felt Pete shift, and stepped back down on the block.

"It's okay, Pete's not going anywhere. He knows you're there. You're doing great."

Tommy placed his left foot back in the stirrup, stood and then swung his right leg over, coming to sit perfectly in the saddle.

"See? Great job! How's it feel?"

Tommy grinned. "Pretty good, but high."

Meredith nodded. "Pete's a tall horse."

"He is, isn't he?" Tommy puffed up his chest a bit. The kid had conquered his fear. For now.

Meredith quickly went over how to position his heels, hips and shoulders. "Okay, now rest your hands on the horn and we'll start walking."

Tommy did so.

"Ready?"

"I am."

"Good, here we go." Meredith walked with Pete through the newly built breezeway into the arena.

Jace was already there, riding Bella around the edge, whispering sweet words of what a good horse she was. It made Meredith smile.

Evening sunlight streamed through the western-side windows. There was still plenty of light coming in from the panels surrounding the top, too. She didn't need to turn on any lights, and joy swelled within her. She'd waited a long time for this and now, there would be so much more she could do with her therapy sessions. She could finally concentrate on growing her client list. This grand opening would show Rose River what she was made of. Would this town rally around her nonprofit or would they reject it? Reject her?

She didn't want to fail.

Glancing at Jace, guilt suddenly swamped her. Had she failed him by relying too much on his willingness to volunteer? He'd helped in so many ways—her house, the grand opening and, of course, Tommy. Jace was also benefiting from these sessions even if his was basically self-guided. His involvement here might not be a normal dynamic since he was her builder, but Jace had counseled her when it came to her parents far more than she had him. Still, part of her felt like she'd crossed the line.

Slowly, she walked Pete around, temporarily lost in her dismal thoughts, but she could feel Tommy relax. She let out the lead rope a little more and watched Tommy in the saddle. He moved well, and didn't slouch. This would be good for him on so many levels, both physically and emotionally.

"Great job, Tommy. You have a good seat, which means you're riding well," she said.

"This is great!" Tommy grinned as he stroked Pete's neck.

"I think so, too," Meredith said.

"I'm proud of you, buddy." Jace maneuvered Bella alongside of Pete.

"And you just learned how to ride?" Tommy asked.

"I did. Miss Meredith is a good instructor." There was admiration in his expression as he glanced at her. Even fondness.

It made her breath hitch. She was in too deep. Against her better judgment, she'd let them become friends, and now, she wanted more. Something she shouldn't have with Jace while he continued in these sessions. If anyone in her line of work found out how Jace had benefited from them, they could make a case against her. RR Equine Therapy would be doomed. And so would she.

The following week, Jace pulled into Meredith's driveway with enough scrap lumber and plywood in the back of his truck to build a small stage. The band preferred playing up, off the sand-based floor in the arena, so here he was. It wouldn't take long to construct a low platform.

He'd taken the afternoon off to help set up for tomorrow's grand opening and a surge of pride filled him. They'd been planning this event for the last month and God had blessed them with a nice weather forecast. People would show. They had to.

Jace noticed a familiar silver car and frowned. He was hoping for some time alone with Meredith before her mother arrived, but that wasn't going to happen. No sense grumbling about it, especially since he'd cheered Meredith on for inviting her parents. Life was too short for them to remain estranged.

He got out of his truck just as Meredith was coming down the steps of her back porch, her mother following close behind her. "Hey."

She stopped and smiled. "Hi, Jace. Thanks for coming. You remember my mom."

How could he forget? "Of course. Hello, Jerrilyn."

"Hello, Jace." The woman gave him a quick smile then nodded toward the house. "There's a box of paper goods in the kitchen, if you wouldn't mind grabbing it. We're heading for the tent."

"Sure. I'll get it." Jace glanced at Meredith but she was already heading down toward the arena, big box in hand.

He stared after her, taking in all that had been done so far. Meredith had rented a tent, tables and chairs and those had all been set up outside, in front of the arena on the crushed-stone parking area. A flat-top grill was positioned just outside the tent. He wondered whom she had to man that grill.

He grabbed the large box Jerrilyn had referenced, then walked it down the slight slope toward the stable and arena, and set it on one of the tables.

Meredith peeked out of the arena door and waved him over. "Jace, come see."

He felt himself smile as he followed her to the automatic garage door, which was open, with the gate pulled across it. Both Bella and Pete were standing close, looking in with interest.

He gave each horse a pet. "Big doings tomorrow. Are you two ready for it?"

"I'll keep them in their stalls. People will want to pet them, and it'll be safer for everyone that way." Meredith stood next to him. She stroked Pete, while he focused on Bella.

He looked at her. "Pretty exciting, huh? We're finally here."

Meredith nodded. "I've been praying for this opportunity a long time."

"God's given you this chance."

"I don't want to mess it up." She looked away.

He stepped closer, but didn't reach for her. He wanted to. Oh, how he wanted to. "You won't. Why would you?"

"Just nervous." She shrugged, stepped back and pointed. "The band will set up at that end, I think. Close to the outlets. We've got enough amperage, right?"

The arena and stable were now on their own line and breaker box. The billing would be separate, too, under RR Equine Therapy. "It's fine, yes. Plenty of power available. And there's no need to be nervous. Everything will be great. Plus, I've got your back."

He meant that. He'd do everything he possibly could to make sure tomorrow was a success. He'd meet and greet, and promote her program. The arena would speak for itself, and Meredith had agreed to leave the built-by-Three Sons Construction sign in place. Good word of mouth for them.

Meredith looked troubled though. She smiled, but it didn't reach her eyes. "Thanks, Jace. Thanks for doing all this. The bandleader, Mitch, assured me they have all their own heavy-duty extension cords. I can't wait to hear them play live. They're good."

"I know." Jace nodded. "You'll save me a dance?"

She looked away. "I hadn't even thought about dancing."

"We'll open up the floor." Delighted by the pink flush of her cheeks, he gently knocked her shoulder with his own.

"I don't think that would be wise."

"Why?"

"I don't want any issues with a perceived conflict of interest on display."

Surely, they were past all that. He'd opened up with her, because they were friends. Okay, her horse had got him started, as well as her instructions to Tommy, but Tommy Tuesdays had always centered on Tommy. They'd never been about him.

"Meredith, where's the conflict? You didn't 'counsel me.'" He made quotes with his fingers. "I simply opened myself up to memories and feelings that I'd stuffed down deep."

Her gaze was steady, as if she was weighing what he said.

"So that's what's bothering you? The whole ethics thing?"

She looked away. "Well, yeah. It's serious. My credentials could be compromised—"

"By who?"

She bit her bottom lip. "My coworkers are invited, as well as area school counselors."

"I'm your builder, your volunteer and your friend. I'm not your client. You refused me, remember?" He reached for her hands and gently shook them. "Don't worry, okay? Everything will turn out great."

"Okay."

Hoping that settled it, he let go and looked around. "I'll get started on the stage. I'm going to back my truck up to those west-side windows. If you'll open them, I can unload everything through there."

"Those big windows are going to be convenient in many ways. I'm glad you suggested them."

She looked more relaxed, as if she'd finally heard him. But did she believe him? He hoped so. He grinned then. "Of course."

Meredith started opening the windows. "I can help you with the stage."

"That will make it go faster, thank you. What about your mom?"

"She's getting the tables covered for now, and setting up the face-painting station. We already moved my patio table, chairs and umbrella in place."

He hadn't noticed that, but then there was a lot to take in. "Who's manning the grill I saw by the tent?"

"Liza's mom and dad. It's just hot dogs. I have chips, too, and a small horse trough will be filled with ice for water and pop. Liza's mom has a huge electric coffee urn she's bringing, so we're covered there, too. My mom and I will bake cookies later tonight."

"Nice." Jace considered what she might have spent on all this and knew it hadn't been cheap. Hopefully, the grand opening would pay off for her program. Hopefully, it would benefit them both with new customers. "What about the silent auction?"

"I've got a long table in the breezeway where I'll attach sheets of paper with each item listed and lines where people can place their bid and leave their contact information. They don't need to be present to win."

"Perfect." Jace would keep things moving as master of ceremonies, but there wouldn't be that much to do. The event was only a three-hour gig in the middle of a Saturday afternoon. It should allow plenty of time for folks to stop by, see the grounds and meet Meredith. Hopefully, they'd see what she did here and support her. He'd prayed for this and for her.

"Before you get your truck, do you want to see the posters in the stable?"

"I sure do." He followed her through the breezeway.

"They came out really well. Signed off on by each of my clients' parents, too." Meredith stepped back to give him room to look closely. "It was a great idea, so thank you for thinking of it."

"Of course." Jace spotted only four posters on the walls, but they were huge, with black-and-white photos of clients smiling out from the glossy paper with either Pete or Bella standing by. Recommendations for Meredith's program had been written in their own words. "Nice."

"This one is my very first client—she was thrilled that I'd asked her for a recommendation."

He touched each one as he read the comments until he came to the poster with a picture of Tommy sitting astride Pete.

Jace drew closer to read what the kid wrote with a scrawling hand.

When I first came to RR Equine Therapy, I wished I could disappear. I didn't want to re-hash what I felt, cuz I didn't feel much anymore. But meeting a horse named Pete helped me feel stuff that was good instead of bad. Miss Meredith helped me learn how to ride Pete, which made me feel really good. And proud. She said you can't let fear of getting hurt keep you from feeling good things and doing good things. She's right.

A lump of emotion thickened his throat. He had to swallow a couple times before he could speak. Jace finally turned toward Meredith, who watched him. "Sounds like a pretty wise kid."

"I know." Her voice was soft.

He reached for one of Meredith's two red braids, and felt the thick softness of her hair twined within. Looking into her eyes, he wanted them to follow that advice, too. He didn't want the fear of loss or her ethical concerns to get in the way of the good things he might have with the woman in front of him. "Meredith, I—"

"Merry— Oh, sorry, I didn't mean to interrupt."

Jace stepped back, frustrated, but then he'd planned to wait until after the grand opening before asking her out. "She was just showing me the posters. They're great."

Jerrilyn smiled, but her eyes held concern mixed with mistrust. "They are good. I had no idea this was so helpful."

Was Meredith's mom finally seeing the light?

"Mom, will you help us unload Jace's truck? He's going to build a platform for the band." Meredith's face was pink again and she wouldn't look at him.

"Sure, honey. I'd love to help." Jerrilyn's gaze narrowed on him, as if she'd saved her daughter in the nick of time.

"Sounds like a plan." Jace headed for his truck, wondering what on earth he'd done to make Meredith's mom look at him as if he was an enemy.

It didn't take long to finish the platform. After she and her mom had helped Jace unload, there hadn't been much for them to do other than hand

Jace tools and hold boards in place while he secured them. The entire time, Meredith couldn't get Jace's words that he wasn't her client out of her head. He was right, of course, but it didn't feel that way.

During sessions, her focus *had* been on Tommy. Jace simply went through the exercises. Meredith hadn't broken down anything with Jace afterward. They hadn't even discussed what he'd processed during those sessions. Had he been a client, she'd have done a poor job. So maybe—

"That should do it." Jace stood back and surveyed his work. The stage wasn't high, just a step up off the sand.

"I'm going to start dinner. Jace, are you staying?" Jerrilyn asked from the doorway.

Jace glanced at her. "Thank you, but no. It's my night to cook at home."

Meredith swallowed her disappointment, watching her mom leave. It was likely better that Jace be on his way. She stepped onto the platform and walked on it. "It's solid."

"Did you expect anything less?" Jace teased.

"No, of course not." Meredith laughed, feeling like maybe everything would be okay. Maybe after tomorrow, they'd stay friends. Maybe after Tommy Tuesdays, they might even go out. She wasn't under a microscope other than her own worries and knowledge that Jace had once asked to be a client.

Jace brushed off his hands. "Want some help putting hay bales around the arena for seating?"

"That'd be great." Meredith nodded. "I have a hand truck in the stable."

"Let's get to it." He was already heading toward the breezeway.

Meredith followed. She didn't want to keep him longer than needed on a late Friday afternoon, when he'd be here most of the day tomorrow. "So what are you making for dinner?"

"Grilling burgers. Nothing fancy. What about you?"

"Mom's making spaghetti."

"Nice. That's one of my favs. I'm sorry to miss it."

Meredith grabbed the hand truck she often used for moving hay and positioned it for loading. "I'll have to make it sometime."

He gave her that warm smile of his. "I look forward to it."

Meredith ignored the flip of her belly and got to work. They managed to wrestle several hay bales into place for seating along the perimeter of the arena, keeping the middle open for dancing, should anyone care to dance.

Once finished, Meredith surveyed everything. The arena looked good. Bright and welcoming. She kept thinking about Jace dancing and the question slipped out. "So...you dance?"

He grinned at her. "I'm pretty good. Especially at line dancing."

Meredith wasn't. She'd never even tried it. She'd gone to a few dances in high school, and some college parties had dancing, but never line dancing. She forced a smile. "Well, I'll have to watch you."

He frowned. "So you're sticking with the conflict-of-interest thing."

Meredith nodded. It was safer that way. She'd be safer. "For now, yes."

"Suit yourself." He kicked at the sand floor. "Need help feeding the horses?"

"No, I'll do it later with my mom."

"You two seem more comfortable with each other."

Meredith nodded. "She's trying and so am I. I mean, she's here. That's a good start."

Jace kicked at the floor again. "Good. I guess I'll head home and fire up the grill. Tell your mom thanks for the invite. You two probably have a lot of catching up to do."

"We do." Meredith walked with him out of the arena.

At his truck, Jace opened the door but turned toward her before climbing in. "It's going to be a good day, Merry."

Hearing him say her nickname turned the butterflies loose in her belly. It would always remind her of that first kiss.

She took a quick step back. "I'll see you tomorrow."

"Tomorrow." He gave her a wink, then got in and started the engine.

Meredith waved as he backed out of her driveway. She hoped he was right. She hoped tomorrow was a good day and an even better turnout. She needed the support of Rose River if RR Equine Therapy was ever going to grow. And she needed to show this community that she was a professional who did things the right way. The ethical way. And that meant no dancing with her handsome builder.

Chapter Thirteen

The next morning dawned clear and warm. Perfect for an outdoor event in late September. Perfect for her grand opening. Meredith and her mom had tidied up all the loose ends before breakfast, and now, Meredith stood outside watching the sun play peekaboo with the clouds as the band arrived to set up. She showed them where to plug in and the guys were psyched to have a platform for their musical equipment, compliments of Jace.

Jace. He crept into her thoughts constantly.

As she came out of the arena, Meredith spotted him in his truck. He'd just pulled into the yard area they'd sectioned off on the other side of her driveway. She chuckled at how much room they'd made and hoped it would be even halfway full.

"Morning!" He grinned at her.

It was only eleven, so most of the morning was gone.

"Good morning," she called out, walking toward him. He looked good as always, but today he'd dressed in a pair of newer jeans and a navy pullover with a small Three Sons Construction logo in white over his heart. Of course, he'd want to be identified as the builder while milling around. And that reminded her that she needed to change her clothes.

When Jace stood before her, he gave her a once-over. "Is that what you're wearing?"

"No. Of course not." She laughed.

"Good, because as cute as that Superman T-shirt is on you, it's seen better days."

She sucked in a breath when he stepped closer and lifted a braid from her shoulder.

"What about your hair?" The dark blue of his shirt made his eyes seem even darker.

Searching his gaze, she stepped back, nervous. Since when did he start looking at *her* like that— like she was attractive, maybe even *beautiful*? She covered up her surprise with a joke. "What are you, my stylist now?"

"Is that a problem?" he replied with a saucy wink.

Her stomach flipped. Should she play along? It might be fun. He was just teasing her, caught up in the excitement of the day.

"That depends on what you're planning to do." She flipped back her braid and was floored by his darkened gaze.

"I'd love to see it loose," he said softly.

The hum of awareness buzzed around them, and Meredith swallowed. He wasn't kidding. He was serious. And she was in over her head in this flirtatious game. "It's a frizzy mess."

"Let me be the judge of that." His tone coaxed her.

Her knees were weakening and she might just melt on the spot if she wasn't careful. "We'll see. Now, can you go check on the band and make sure they won't blow a fuse with their equipment plugged in?"

He grinned. "Not happening. You could run indoor heaters if you wanted, but I'll make sure, just the same."

"Thank you." Meredith breathed easier. Whatever had sizzled between them had been extinguished. She headed for the house to change, looked up and spotted her mom in the kitchen window, frowning.

Now what?

Her mother had been a huge help, but Meredith wasn't sure if she had her mom's full support. While making the dozens and dozens of chocolate chip cookies last night, her mother kept asking about her plan B, as if expecting her program to fail. That hadn't helped Meredith's fears over that very thing. What if she failed to raise awareness, and no one bid on the auction items? What if this whole day turned out to be one big flop?

Meredith stepped into the kitchen and spotted her mother's overnight bag by the door. "I'm going upstairs to get ready. Do you need help with anything?"

"No. I'm good. I'll stay for the first hour, then head home."

It's what they'd agreed to. Meredith's father planned to arrive around two. The grand opening would run from one o'clock until four, but folks might show up early, too. She gave her mother a hug. "Thank you for everything."

"You're welcome."

Meredith pulled back, but her mother stalled her with a light touch to her arm.

"Be careful with that guy."

Here it comes. "Jace?"

Her mom nodded.

"Why, Mom? What's wrong with him?"

Her mom briefly closed her eyes, then opened them with a look of pity. "He's just not right for you."

Meredith's hackles went up. "Why not?"

"Do I really have to spell it out for you?"

"Maybe you do," she answered cooly.

"Look at him, Merry. He could have his pick of women. Why would he stay with you?"

Meredith involuntarily jerked like she'd been slapped. Hadn't she thought the same thing? But this was her mother pointing it out as if it were so obvious. As if history was destined to repeat itself.

"I'm only trying to protect you." Her mom

touched her arm again, softly stroking her skin. "You know, from what I went through."

Meredith held her breath in order to control the wave of hurt that battered her, threatening to pull her under. After spending a great evening together last night, she had to ruin it with this. Maybe her mom didn't believe in her abilities. Maybe she never would. "Don't worry, Mom. We're just friends."

Meredith left it at that and ran upstairs to change. As she rummaged through her closet, hot tears burned her eyes. Part of her believed her mother, but part of her rebelled, too. For once in her life, Meredith wished she could get the guy she wanted and keep him. Was that so terrible?

Looking in the mirror, Meredith pulled the hair tie from her braid and slowly unwound her hair. Dare she? It was now or never. It was time to wear her hair loose to see how Jace reacted. He might prove both her and her mother wrong.

Jace spotted Meredith from a distance and stopped in his tracks. The scripture about a woman's long hair described as her glory raced through his mind. He'd never seen hair more glorious than Meredith's. Her crinkled red tresses flowed down around her shoulders and swept to the middle of her back.

She walked toward him wearing a soft-looking sweater that puddled over a long skirt that fluttered around her boots. He never took his eyes off her. He couldn't.

She finally stood before him with a shy smile. "Well?"

"You have definitely got some hair." Jace kept staring.

A shadow crossed her face. "Told you. It's a frizzy mess."

"No. It's not." He tipped his head to see that she had some of it pulled to the back of her head, anchored with a clip. "It's incredible."

"Good or bad?" Meredith muttered, then raised her hand. "Never mind, maybe I'd rather not—"

He took both her hands in his to stop her rambling. "Meredith."

She looked at him.

"You're beautiful inside and out."

For a long moment she held his gaze, then sighed and looked beyond him. "That's Liza and her folks. I better help them get set up."

He let her go. Why didn't she believe him? What had he done to make her think he wouldn't be truthful when he gave her a compliment? He wasn't blowing smoke. He'd meant every word. Jace walked down the slope to the arena. He could hear the band gearing up and approached them.

Stepping inside, he watched for a second or two while they tuned their instruments. "Hey, Mitch." Jace walked forward. "Do you guys want to wait for people to arrive before you play, or just get right into it?"

"We'll play. You can give us an intro after we take a break, like when there's a good crowd."

Jace nodded. "Anything other than what we talked about?"

"Nope, that's good. Just make sure to announce that we're playing at Charlie's later tonight at nine."

"Got it." Jace headed for the stable to check on Bella and Pete. Antsy for something to do, he grabbed a scoop of grain from the bin in the tack room and then stepped into Pete's stall. He'd split the scoop between the two horses. "Here you go, Pete."

Jace stroked the gelding's neck before moving on into Bella's stall. She nudged his arm with her nose, then tried to eat the grain from the scoop. He chuckled and dumped the contents into the rubber feeding bowl affixed to the wall.

"Don't tell Meredith that I'm giving you guys a treat," he whispered as he stroked the dark mare's mane, threading his fingers through the thick strands. "Ah, Bella, thank you for helping me to finally look inside myself."

He may have grown up in a Christian household where his father had read a passage of scripture every morning before they went to school, but Jace hadn't really surrendered his heart to God. Recently, he'd done just that, and it was as if God had led him here, to this horse and the woman who owned her. Being around Bella, Jace had let himself feel the loss of his parents once again. This time, he felt as if he'd finally accepted it. He'd been running from that for so long, filling his free time with women who had distracted him from doing what needed to be done.

He hung out with the horses a while longer, listening to the band play. He should mill around and represent his family business, but he cherished this moment with the horses, with Bella, and decided to stay just a little longer. By the sounds of cars and chatter he heard coming through the open doors of the stable, people had arrived early. Surely, that boded well for the event.

"Is that Jace Moore?"

Jace cringed at the sound of a familiar feminine voice. He exited the stall and turned to face a woman he'd never have expected to see here, of all places. She was from a time in his life he wasn't proud of. "Hi, Bailey, what are you doing here?"

She gave him a wide smile. "I just moved to Rose River. Hired in as the new librarian. Finally, something full-time."

"Good for you." Bailey had been a part-time bartender as well as a library assistant when he'd met her. She was stunning, but her looks held no allure for him. Not anymore.

She walked toward him with purpose in her gaze.

He stepped back and connected with the stall behind him, trapped.

"So…" She ran her finger across the top of the stall door. "Maybe, we can get together and bring each other up to speed."

"I'm sort of seeing someone—" If Meredith agreed to go out with him for real.

Just then, Jace heard footsteps and looked over Bailey's shoulder to see Meredith leading a small group of people through the stable.

Her gaze connected with his and her blue eyes widened when she spotted Bailey.

"We'll be on our way." He reached for Bailey's arm and steered her toward the breezeway. He could only imagine what Meredith might be thinking, but the last thing she needed was the two of them in the way of a tour. And he didn't want Meredith to overhear Bailey ask him a bunch of questions. "Come, listen to the band."

"Gladly." Bailey looped her arm in his.

He glanced back, but Meredith kept talking, introducing the people with her to Bella and Pete. She didn't look his way.

"So tell me about this girl you're seeing." Bailey's voice sounded tight, but at least she wasn't loud.

"Well—" When they entered the arena, a few people had already formed a square for line dancing.

Bailey pulled him into their midst. "Remember this?"

"Of course." Line dancing at the bar and grill

where she worked, where they'd met, was one of their weekly activities. Jace didn't want to make a scene and refuse her. It was only a line dance after all, not a big deal.

At least, he hoped it wouldn't be.

The grand opening was in full swing and Meredith couldn't be more pleased with the turnout. Several of her coworkers from Hillman attended and she recognized many folks from town. A couple of waitresses from the Rose River Café, ladies from the library and even Sam, the owner of the hardware store, showed up with his family.

Jace mingled like a pro, introduced the band and invited all to take part in the silent auction. She'd see him here and there, but right now he kicked up his heels in the arena. He was good at line dancing and several women, both old and young, had clustered around him. But the image of him standing close to the beautiful blonde when she'd entered the stable pricked at her thoughts over and over. They obviously knew each other, and most likely had a history. The memory plagued her like a deeply embedded sliver, a sore spot in an otherwise perfect day.

Clenching her hands into fists, Meredith strolled out of the arena toward the face-painting table. Liza didn't have anyone there, so Meredith asked, "How's the cosmetic supplies? Do you need anything?"

Liza smiled back. "The makeup is fine, but I could use a hot dog with mustard."

"You got it." Meredith crossed the path and swung by the grill manned by Liza's dad. The juicy aroma coming off that flat top made her belly growl. She fished two cans of pop out of the icy trough and slipped them into the pockets of her skirt. The cold, wet cans made her shiver in spite of the warm day.

She asked Liza's dad, "Got two that are well done?"

"I do. The dogs are going fast, but I see you have plenty in the cooler yet."

Liza's mom held out two buns cradled in napkins for her husband to fill then handed them to Meredith. "Here you go, honey."

"When they're gone, they're gone. No worries." She turned to squirt a line of mustard along the middle of both dogs. "Thank you both for doing this. If you need a break, let me know. I can fill in."

"Oh, no, we're fine. It's fun."

Meredith glanced at Liza's dad, rolling hot dogs along the hot surface. She wasn't sure he was having that much fun, but she was beyond grateful that they'd volunteered. "I owe you both big-time."

"Not at all." Liza's mom waved her away with a smile. "Our donation to the cause."

"And very appreciated." Meredith walked back to the face-painting station, handed over a hot dog, then the can of cola to Liza. "Here you go."

"Thanks," Liza said. "Great turnout so far."

"Yes, better than I expected." Meredith bit into her hot dog and looked around. Silence settled over them as they wolfed down the dogs.

"How come you're not dancing? I saw Jace out there." Liza nodded toward the arena.

Meredith finished chewing her last bite. She couldn't tell Liza the real reason she wouldn't dance with Jace, but managed a good excuse. "My father should be here soon, so I'm keeping an eye out for him."

Her father had agreed to come, but she never really knew when it came to her dad. He might not show.

All the doors to the stable and arena were open, as well as the windows, so the sounds of the band and people either singing along or clapping to the music could be clearly heard. It definitely gave the event a party atmosphere. A fun party. She hoped that sent the right message.

Meredith stuffed her hands into her skirt pockets to keep from wringing them.

Liza nodded. "I've seen Jace working the crowd like he owns the place. He's so proud of all this, and I overheard him singing your praises to someone on the school board. Can't remember the guy's name, only the face. That's how I know he's on the school board."

"Are they still here?" Meredith would love to make a connection into Rose River's high school.

Liza had passed along her information to the school counselor, along with business cards, eons ago, but nothing had come of it. Higher-up recognition could really help with referrals.

"I don't know. You might want to ask Jace."

"I'll do that."

Liza stalled her with a light touch. "He's different, Meredith. He's more open or something, and I think it's because of you."

Meredith's lips parted with pleasant surprise. Was Liza giving her stamp of approval? She wanted to talk more but stepped aside as a group of three giggly, grade-school-age girls approached Liza to have their faces painted. And Meredith needed to find that school board member. "Thanks, Liza."

"Of course." Her friend shoved the last bite of her hot dog into her mouth and then sanitized her hands with antibacterial wipes before waving the girls over.

Meredith headed for the arena to find Jace. She'd been avoiding him ever since she had seen him in the stable. So much for trying to get the guy; she'd lost his attention pretty fast.

She looked around for Jace and spotted him talking to an older couple near his construction company's sign. Jace's brother John was there, too. She walked toward them.

Jace spotted her and smiled, excused himself and met her halfway.

She tried to ignore the way her spine tingled as he drew close. "Hey."

"Success, huh? Have you seen the silent auction lists? They're practically full."

"There's a second sheet underneath." Meredith pushed her hair back from the breeze that teased it forward.

Jace smiled again.

And that uncomfortable tingling sensation took over again, making Meredith suddenly cross. "Did you happen to talk to someone from the school board?"

"I did."

Meredith looked around. "Are they still here?"

"They are not."

"I wish you would have found me, I—"

He pulled a business card out of his back pocket and handed it to her. "He'd like you to call him during the week to go over your program. He wants to pursue placing you on their list for counselor referrals of students to therapists."

"Really?" Excitement replaced irritation as she took the card and slipped it into her skirt pocket. This was exactly what she'd been hoping for. Looking into Jace's kind eyes, she finally said, "Thank you."

The breeze teased strands of her hair forward again, and this time Jace pushed them back, tucking them behind her ear. "Told you this would be a good thing, for both you and me. That couple I was talking to want an estimate on a barn. John's going to meet with them tomorrow. And Jeremy's here with friends to hear the band. A couple of them have placed bids, too."

"Good. I'm glad. Jace—" Should she even ask about that woman in the stable? No. She wouldn't. It was none of her business, anyway, whom he saw or didn't see. They were friends, and *she'd* requested they remain that way.

Just then, her attention was grabbed by a tall man with dark hair liberally streaked with gray. Her father was walking beside a woman who looked only a few years older than Meredith.

He spotted her and waved.

She waved back.

"Who's that?" Jace asked.

"That is my father," Meredith answered. "I have no idea who's with him. A new girlfriend, perhaps."

Jace narrowed his gaze and muttered under his breath. "A little young…"

Of course, she agreed, but didn't say anything. Her father had never married the woman he'd left her mother over. In fact, they hadn't lasted more than a year. Her father had moved on to another, and then another until Meredith had lost count.

"Hello, Meredith," he said.

"Hello, Daddy. This is Jace Moore, the contractor who built the arena."

"Greg Lewis." Her father extended his hand to

Jace, who returned the handshake. "From here, it looks like a nice job on that arena."

"Good to meet you, sir, and thanks. Your daughter directed the plans." Jace looked expectantly toward the woman, waiting for an introduction.

It never came. And before Meredith could even turn to the woman, her father said, "Give me a tour, Meredith. We don't have much time."

Of course, he didn't. When had he ever? But then, what had she expected? Change didn't happen overnight. "Where are you headed?"

"Mackinac Island. We have reservations." Her father was already in motion, moving toward the arena.

He'd never taken his own daughter there. Swallowing resentment that bubbled into her throat, Meredith turned to the woman. "Hi, I'm Meredith."

The woman smiled. "My name is Tracy. It's very nice to meet you."

Meredith nodded, knowing whatever relationship they had, it wouldn't last. Did Tracy know that? Did she even care?

Meredith glanced back to see if Jace was coming with them, but he remained standing with an odd expression on his face. Irritation took over. She didn't want his pity. She didn't need it. In fact, she didn't need him or anyone else. Her parents were a prime reminder that other than God's provision, the only person she could rely on was herself.

Chapter Fourteen

Jace stepped onto the platform, taking over the microphone from Mitch. "We'd like to thank you all for coming today. Wasn't the band great?" Once the applause died down, Jace added. "You can hear them again tonight at Charlie's starting at nine o'clock."

He looked for Meredith and spotted her gathering up the silent auction forms. "Meredith Lewis, the owner of RR Equine Therapy, is going to close out the event by announcing the silent auction winners."

She wasn't close enough to the stage, so Jace kept talking. "I want you to know that Meredith's program can have an even broader impact with your support. Her sessions have changed lives and her horses are amazing animals. Being around them has certainly helped me. So let me turn it over to Ms. Lewis."

While the audience applauded again, he noticed that the color had drained from Meredith's face. She stood motionless for a second or two, clutching the auction sheets to her chest. Surely, she wasn't succumbing to stage fright. They'd agreed that she'd close out the event this way.

He gave her a coaxing nod.

She moved quickly onto the stage and took the microphone from him. "Thank you, Jace. My builder, everyone."

More applause. He grinned, glad for the recognition, and stepped off the platform.

Meredith took a deep breath before continuing. "I'd like to thank you all again for coming. I look forward to serving this community and my special thanks go to those who donated their goods and services for the auction. As you know, Three Sons Construction built this arena, and they've graciously donated their labor for a roof replacement. The winner of that service is…"

Whatever had shaken Meredith at first was gone. With her usual composure, she announced each winner and clapped along with the rest of them. She rattled off the instructions for those present to pick up their prize from her, thanked everyone again and the event was officially over.

While Meredith met with the silent auction winners, Jace helped the band load up their instruments. He walked toward the grill, hoping for a hot dog, but Liza and her parents were cleaning up.

"Sorry, Jace, everything's gone," Liza said as she loaded condiments into a cooler.

"That's okay." He shrugged. "It went well, don't you think?"

She gave him a soft smile. "It did. Thank you for helping Meredith. She needed you."

"My pleasure." Jace winked.

Liza shook her head. "I'm going to set this on the back porch and then head out with my folks. Let Meredith know, okay?"

"Sure thing." Jace may have given his usual, corny response, but he couldn't deny the warmth that filled him when he heard that Meredith needed him.

They made a good team, the two of them. He wanted to be there for Meredith, meeting her needs as she met his. Maybe now, after coming to terms with the loss of his parents, he might be the kind of man who'd stick around. He'd never know until he tried, and that meant asking Meredith to go out with him for real.

After stripping off the paper coverings from the tables, Jace shoved them into a garbage can that was already full. He tamped everything down, pulled up the sides of the liner bag and tied it off. There were more garbage pails that needed emptying in the stable and arena, so he headed that way.

He couldn't get Meredith's parents out of his thoughts. Between her bitter mother and dismissive father, it was no wonder Meredith had needed Bella growing up. He couldn't help but be grateful for the parents he'd had, even though it was much too short a time.

He heard music coming from the stable area and entered through the opened arena door. He caught a glimpse of Meredith's skirt as she ducked around the corner, out of his line of vision. A song by Coldplay came on from the nearby radio. A song he knew well. The lyrics of "A Sky Full of Stars" were appropriate in so many ways. He could sing them to Meredith and mean every word, especially now. But he didn't sing.

He walked up behind her and circled her waist. Feeling her turn, he pulled her into his arms and swayed with the music. "We never danced today."

She swayed, too, but her blue eyes narrowed. Their color looked as cold as a winter sky. "You didn't lack for partners."

"True. Dance with me now." He twirled her out and then brought her back in against his chest and went into a two-step. Meredith followed his lead. She was light on her feet, making him regret that they hadn't partnered up for the live band.

A smile hovered around her mouth. He wanted those lips under his own, but should wait until he'd officially asked her. "Go out with me."

"No." She pulled back.

"Why not?" He saw a flash of anger heat what had been so chilly before.

"You just admitted in front of everyone that you're as good as my client."

"I did?" When had he done that?

"You admitted that the horses really helped you."

"So what?" He grinned. "That doesn't mean anything."

"With all the counselors around, it sure could. And I could get in trouble. Fired."

"Wait, what? Why? We're friends." Only he didn't want to be just friends any longer.

"Yeah, and that's a problem, too. I shouldn't get personally involved with a client for two years after termination of services. And if anyone thinks you're a client, even though you're not—"

"Whoa, slow down."

She looked at him as if she'd like to terminate him.

Jace held up his hands in surrender. "Look, if it makes you feel better, I'll wait it out." What was he saying?

Meredith snorted with sarcasm. "Right."

The song ended and an annoying commercial jingle started.

He stepped toward her. "This sounds like a lot more than just a perceived conflict of interest."

Meredith looked away. Busted. "Look, it's my hang-up. It has nothing to do with you."

He didn't believe that for a minute. "It has everything to do with me and whatever it is I did today to make you mad."

"I'm not mad." She sighed. "Okay, maybe a

little mad seeing you with that woman in the stable, but—"

"I dated her a long time ago," he interrupted.

"Everywhere we go, you've dated someone."

Guilty as charged. "That might be true, but that was a different time in my life. A time when I looked for distraction. I'm not that same guy."

"But you can date anyone you want—"

"I want you." He said it quietly.

And that declaration seemed to make Meredith more upset instead of less. She let out a bitter laugh he didn't like hearing. It made her sound too much like her mother. "You say that now, but down the road—"

"Down the road, what?" He could feel his temper rising.

"You'll want someone else and leave," she yelled.

He yelled right back, "You don't know that!"

She glared at him.

He lowered his voice. "You haven't even given us a chance."

"I can't."

"Meredith, listen—"

She leaned against the table that had held all the bids for the silent auction. Those papers were neatly stacked now, with a horseshoe set on top. Her eyes begged him to stop. "No, you listen. I don't want to get hurt."

"I don't, either. Hurting you is the last thing I'd ever want to do."

"You don't understand what it's like for me—" Her voice cracked.

He reached for her and softly rubbed her shoulder. She was the professional. Maybe there was something wrong with him that couldn't be fixed. Or maybe something with her. "Then tell me. What makes you so sure I'll hurt you?"

She sighed. "I already told you about the boyfriend in college who dumped me for my roommate—"

"I'm not your old boyfriend." Jace tried to lighten the mood. "Is that all you've got?"

Meredith chuckled, but there was no amusement in the sound. "I wish that was it."

His stomach sank. He wasn't going to like what he heard and braced for it. "Then tell me."

"You've met my parents."

"I have." They were messed up. He clenched his jaw, but nodded for her to go on.

"I was thirteen and at the shopping mall when I saw my father embrace a woman other than my mom. This lady was so beautiful, I remember thinking she looked like a movie star." Meredith paused a moment. "Anyway, at first, I thought maybe they were friends. But then they kissed, and my father caught me staring at them."

Jace felt his hands roll into fists. His impression of her father hadn't been good. Now, he knew the guy was a jerk, but he kept quiet and waited for her to continue.

"I didn't know what to do. I stewed over it for days and then finally, I told my mother. I thought if she confronted my father, he'd stop messing around and that would be that."

"But he didn't, did he?" Jace could easily read the pain in her eyes, the hurt.

"No. He asked for a divorce and my mother blamed me for tattling. She'd said that she could have lived in ignorance of my father's affairs and been okay with that, but since I stirred everything up—" Meredith slumped her shoulders.

Having met her parents, he could see it all unfolding in his mind's eye and his heart broke for her. How could they put that on her?

Keeping his voice soft, he looked her in the eyes. "Meredith, I'm not your father, either. I'd never do that to you."

"No?" Her voice held a challenge. She didn't believe him.

He felt the insult down deep. "No!"

"Jace, your reputation precedes you."

"My reputation—"

She'd put him in the same category as her cheating dad, which was bad enough, but pulling out his past and waving it in his face as if to shame him hurt. It hurt really bad.

Jace ran a hand through his hair and tried to calm down. "Look, it's true, I may have used women as a way to dull the pain, but I never misled or lied to one of them. I never shared who I am, not like I do with you. And God has forgiven me. Why can't you?"

"Jace, it's not that simple." She didn't want to extend forgiveness or trust. Wasn't she in a career that promoted change and second chances?

He *had* changed, and standing here begging her to give them a chance proved it. "It is that simple, Meredith. I lost the two most important people in my life. There isn't a day that goes by that I don't miss them, or wish they were here. Don't you think this might be scary for me, too? You might be the one who leaves me."

"It's *not* that simple, Jace. It can't be." She stared him down.

And that fired him up. "You're a counselor who doesn't believe what she preaches. And you're the one making it complicated."

She had her arms crossed again, trying to block out his words. He might as well talk to the wall. Nothing he'd said was getting through to her. Meredith had years of hurt that she held on to, pulling it around her shoulders like a cape or some kind of shield.

Heaving a sigh, he held out his hands in defeat. "I'm sorry you think so little of me, but I guess you have every right to." He turned to go, but when he reached the arena door, he stopped and looked at her. "God never promised life would be easy. He only asks that we trust Him with the life we have. We can make it Meredith, if we trust

God for real and not just give Him lip service. Then maybe we can learn to trust each other."

She still didn't respond. All that fire in her hair was wasted. She looked cold and distant again. Too afraid to open up her heart and take a chance on him. On them.

"While you're at it, read Tommy's poster again." And then, Jace walked away.

Meredith watched Jace leave. With every fiber of her being, she wanted to run after him, but instead, she remained frozen in place. Was he right? Was she a fraud who couldn't see in herself what she helped with in others? Or maybe Jace was playing her. But that didn't ring true. He'd never steered her wrong. He'd never made empty promises. He'd asked only that she open the dance floor with him and she'd turned him down flat.

Closing her eyes, she remembered the feel of his arms around her only moments ago as they'd swayed to the song on the radio. It had been sheer bliss and complete torture.

Meredith opened her eyes and her gaze landed on the platform that she'd helped Jace construct. Her heart weighed down even more. He'd done so much around here, volunteering for far more than just the horses. He'd fixed things and helped with the grand opening, and yet she'd pushed him away. Maybe for good.

She gathered up the silent auction sheets that

she'd left on the table and ran for the house. She'd
contact the winners that were not present and then
tally up the total of funds raised today. She'd clean
up the rest of everything tomorrow. The tent rental
company was coming in the morning, anyway.

As she stepped into her kitchen, her gaze was
drawn to the sink's leaky faucet Jace had fixed.
And the door to the basement he'd leveled properly, and then there was the screen door he'd attached in front while she'd been at Liza's cabin.
Maybe he *was* a man she could depend on. A man
who wouldn't leave, but might actually make her
an important part of his life. Still, if she took that
risk and he let her down, what then?

She put her hands in her pockets and connected
with the business card of the school's superinten-
dent. She pulled it out, and hot tears burned her
eyes and her throat grew thick. Jace had talked to
the guy with pride.

Why did she think the worst of him when he'd
been nothing but kind to her?

After tossing the papers and business card onto
her dining room table, Meredith ran upstairs. She
had to get out on the trail and clear her mind; everything else could wait.

She'd take Bella out for a quick ride. It wouldn't
be dark for a couple of hours yet and she needed to
get away from seeing Jace everywhere she turned.

After changing, Meredith exited her house and
practically ran to the stables, where Bella and Pete

were still in their stalls. She let Pete out into the pasture, shut the door and then led Bella out of her stall to saddle her up. Heading for the tack room, she walked past Tommy's poster.

She could hear Jace's voice taunting her to re-read it. She knew what the boy had written. She remembered telling Tommy that very thing the day of his first ride. But she looked up and read over the quote again, zeroing in on her own para-phrased words: *You can't let fear of getting hurt keep you from feeling good things and doing good things.*

Ethics aside, was Jace a *good thing*? That was the big question. Could she really step out in faith and trust that he was a good thing? A good man for her, despite her mother's warnings? And even if they didn't stay together, could she trust God to get her through a breakup?

She'd never wanted to experience what her mother had gone through. It was bad enough that her father had left them both, but could she allow herself to love a man who might, one day, do the same thing? Any man was capable of be-trayal, but Jace came with a history of dating so many women. What if she didn't measure up? What if she wasn't enough? She hadn't been rea-son enough to keep her parents together.

"God, how do I trust him?"

Meredith didn't wait for an answer. She got

Bella ready to ride then mounted up and reined her out of the stable.

Pete knickered to go, too.

And Bella danced around as if stalling, getting a last look at Pete in the pasture.

"Not this time, Pete. We'll be back." Meredith clicked her tongue and pressed her knees against Bella's side, pleased when her mare went right into a trot.

Bella knew this was one of those rides. The rides Meredith needed every now and then. As soon as they hit the straightaway of the trail, Bella slipped into a smooth canter. Meredith let the mare have her head and it didn't take much to coax her into an exhilarating gallop. Meredith relaxed, letting her mind wander. As they raced down the trail, she revisited every moment she'd spent with Jace.

Too late, Meredith saw the dark blur of a bear run across the path ahead of them. Her hold on the reins was too loose, her seat too relaxed. Bella saw the bear, too, and spooked. Her mare stopped quickly and turned—and Meredith went flying.

She landed on the ground with a thud and gasped, trying to breathe. With the wind knocked out of her, it took Meredith a few seconds to sit up. When she did, Bella was already down the trail, hightailing it home as if that bear was chomping at her heels.

"Great, just great." Meredith blew out her breath

and patted her back pockets, hoping she didn't break her phone. It wasn't there, and then she remembered that she'd left her phone at home. *Stupid!*

After dragging herself up, she dusted off her backside and started walking. The sun had since set and it'd be dark soon, probably by the time she made it home. She should have been paying more attention while riding. She knew better.

Her foot caught at something and twisted, and down she went again, onto her knees, then her stomach. This time, real pain shot up her left leg. She glanced back and saw the exposed root her foot was still wedged under and nearly howled in frustration.

Could this day get any worse?

No. There were good things about today. A lot of good things.

You can't let fear of getting hurt keep you from feeling good things and doing good things.

In her mind, she heard Tommy's voice, and then Jace's. And it tore her in two. She ground out a prayer. "God, please help me."

She breathed in, trying to fight the tears, but gave up. Lying on the ground, she slammed her fist on the soft sand of the path and wept.

Driving home, Jace fumed. The cool evening air blowing in from the open truck window did nothing to calm his temper. Nor did the sight of the sun, low in the sky, shining through trees with leaves changing from green to gold, orange and red. Those leaves would soon die and fall. Everything faded away to death. Maybe that was a little morose, but it was the reason he didn't get too close. Getting cut loose hurt too much.

Still, how could Meredith lump him in with guys like her father? Why couldn't she see him for who he was inside, instead of what he'd done or who he'd once been? He ran a hand through his hair and blew out a breath.

Classic. The one woman he wanted, didn't want him back.

Wallowing wasn't something he was used to, but self-pity swamped him. He tended to veer away from giving in to feelings, but right now, the overwhelming sense of failure that filled him threatened to flatten him. He'd lost Meredith's regard and, worse, maybe her respect.

His thoughts kept running over their argument and once again, he recalled the stark pain in her eyes when she told him about her parents. She'd been only thirteen when they'd split. A year younger than he'd been when his mom and dad had died. Emotionally, Meredith's parents had turned their backs on her—blaming her, no less, for their divorce. In a way, she'd lost her parents, too.

Was it any wonder that she understood Tommy's plight? The kid lacked confidence in himself and his parents. Meredith seemed to understand Jace, too, although her fear that he'd leave her got in the way. Was he any different? He'd always been afraid to love.

He slowed the truck and pulled off the road, realizing his error more fully. He had blamed her, too. Instead of discerning why she was so afraid, he'd insulted her, practically calling her a fraud. What a numbskull he was and his anger was misplaced.

Meredith needed no more blame or rejection in her life. No more selfish defensiveness. She needed love. Unconditional, full-on love. Could he give her that?

"I can't leave things like this," he muttered and turned the truck around.

This wouldn't keep until tomorrow. Jace had to tell her how he felt *now*. In person. He pushed down the gas pedal, impatient to get back to her.

A few miles down the road, he got stuck behind a slowpoke and beeped the horn in frustration as he waited for oncoming traffic to clear. When it did, he passed the slow vehicle in front of him. His heart pounded and his head felt light. He was giddy with the realization of what he felt. He wasn't going to let his or her fear stand in the way. Whatever it took. However long it took.

He pulled into her driveway and quickly parked next to her truck. Her house looked still inside.

Not a single light shone from those lace-curtained windows.

Jace jogged up the steps of the back porch and knocked on the kitchen door, then opened it and called out, "Meredith?"

No answer.

"Meredith?" He walked inside and looked around. The silent auction sheets were lying on the dining room table along with the business card he'd given her. Next to them was her phone.

She had to be here.

He swept through the living room, then to the base of her stairs to the second floor. He knocked on the wall. "Meredith?"

Still no answer.

If she was napping, she wouldn't appreciate him bounding into her room, but something in his gut told him to check, anyway. The house was too quiet and a shiver of unease went up his spine as he took the stairs two at a time.

He'd never been up here before and gave the space a quick glance—maybe three bedrooms and a full bath—but he poked his head into the room with the door left open. Her cat was lying at the foot of a perfectly made double bed. She wasn't in here.

He scratched behind the cat's ears as he looked around and spotted the skirt Meredith had worn earlier draped over a chair. Tall boots lay on the floor as if she'd kicked them off in a hurry. If

Meredith wasn't in the house, she might be in the arena.

Jace rushed back down the stairs and out the kitchen door. The arena doors, as well as the sliding barn doors to the stable, were still open. It wasn't yet dark, but the sun had set and the shadows of dusk were moving in.

He entered the stable and noticed that both stalls were empty. Turning around, he saw a harness hanging from a lead rope still attached to the wall. Meredith must have gone for a ride. He'd wait. She'd be back soon. Before dark. It'd be dark soon.

Jace ambled into the arena and spotted Pete in the pasture. The tall quarter horse stood several feet away from the gated opening of the arena's huge garage door, but suddenly, Pete's ears perked up and he whinnied. And then, Jace heard Bella neigh in return. Relief filled him. They were back.

He pressed the button to close the big door. Then he moved to the west-side windows and closed them, too. They were in for a cold night ahead, according to the weather forecast. He'd wait for Meredith and Bella and meet them in the stable. After closing the main entrance to the arena, he turned in time to see Bella wander inside from the stable. She was saddled, her reins looped over the saddle horn, but without Meredith.

Bella walked straight toward him.

He took hold of the reins under her chin in one

hand and rubbed her face then her sweat-soaked neck with other, looking for any outward injuries. Finding none, he asked, "Where's Meredith?"

Bella lifted her head and snorted.

The lead ball in his gut grew heavier and his ears thundered with dread. What had happened to Meredith? His hands shook slightly as he led Bella back into the stable. "Come on, girl. Into your stall."

After slipping off her harness once she was safely secured inside, he led Pete into his because it seemed like the right thing to do. With both horses in the stable, Jace took off for his truck at a run. Knowing Bella had returned without her rider scared him like nothing he'd ever wanted to feel. This was why he didn't get close to anyone, but it was too late for that. He was already in the deep end. He loved Meredith.

He prayed she was okay, but the nagging question pounded in his thoughts. Why would an experienced rider like Meredith fall off her horse? Bella was too gentle to throw her, unless something had spooked her. And whatever that might have been, was it still out there with Meredith?

A shiver passed through him, making him hurry. Darkness was settling in as Jace pulled out of the driveway and turned onto the trail with a multi-use marker. He rolled down his window all the way, but couldn't hear any sounds other than small branches scraping against the side of this truck. He flicked on his high-beam headlights, then drove as fast as he dared, but there was no sign of Meredith.

He kept driving and darkness had closed in around him just like the thickness of trees lining the trail created a tunnel in his headlights. And then, he saw something up ahead. A mass of red hair in the path. She wasn't moving and Jace felt like his heart stopped beating. He couldn't breathe.

Dear Lord, please let her be okay.

Then Meredith raised her head and squinted against the glare of the headlights. Relief flooded through him so fast, he thought he'd throw up. Instead, he slammed the truck into Park and hurried out, leaving the door open. He didn't take his eyes off of her. Leaves were stuck in that glorious mane, and her eyes in the bright lights looked puffy.

As he got closer, Jace noticed her mascara was smeared and she'd been crying. Was she hurt and if so, how badly?

Chapter Fifteen

A tremor ran through Meredith as a man got out of that truck. A tall, dark silhouette. She couldn't see much else through the brightness of those high-beam headlights. She tensed and then sucked in her breath as another sharp stab of pain in her ankle sliced through her.

"Meredith?"

Hearing his voice, she breathed easier. "Jace? Is that you?"

He was kneeling beside her now. "Are you hurt?"

She tried to turn over and sit up, but her foot was wedged in tight under that root. "My foot is caught and I twisted my ankle. Other than that, I'm okay."

"And you left your phone on the dining room table," he scolded.

"I know. That was dumb."

He squeezed her shoulder as he shifted down near her foot. Feeling just above her ankle through her jeans and boot, he gingerly touched all the way down. "I can't tell if anything's broken, but I don't want to risk it by pulling your foot out. I've got a small saw in the truck."

"Saw?" Meredith closed her eyes. He'd need the lights on to see, but they were blinding, giving her a headache.

"To cut your foot free," he called from the truck. He was back in seconds and quietly began sawing through the root.

She gritted her teeth when his knuckles grazed the inside of her ankle. Why was he here?

"Sorry," he whispered.

But her foot was finally free. She rolled over and went up on all fours, testing her strength, but her left boot felt tight and her ankle throbbed. "I think my ankle is swollen."

"Can you stand?"

"I don't know. I'll try." She kneeled now, and braced for pain. It came in a hot, sharp wave that made her nauseous.

Jace scooped her up, then gently shifted her into his arms. "Let's get you seated in the truck instead of on the cold ground."

The warmth of his arms and breath seeped into her and she shivered. The night air had turned chilly and the lightweight sweater she wore was useless. She started to shake in earnest.

"Just a little farther." Jace managed to open the passenger side door with her still in his arms.

He set her on the seat, facing him instead of the windshield.

She hiked herself up a little farther back with her good foot, letting her left leg dangle. The overhead light was on and Jace's face looked pale, his expression tense as he lifted the pantleg of her jeans.

She grimaced. It hurt.

"Sorry," he said again. He felt up and down her boot, looking for a zipper. "I don't want to hurt you."

"These are pull-on," Meredith explained.

"Great. That means I have to pull them off or cut them off." Jace stood up and stretched out his back, then gave her a teasing wink. "You know, you're heavier than you look."

She knew he was trying to lighten the moment. He looked worried. No, more than that. He looked rattled. And she couldn't seem to verbalize the things running through her thoughts. Funny, that their argument had been about who would hurt whom in the end. Cradled in his arms moments ago, she'd felt safe and warm. That had to speak for something.

Plus, he'd come back. *Why?* "Were you at the house? Did you see Bella?"

"I put her and Pete in their stalls. They're fine. I took off Bella's harness, but I'll take care of her saddle when we get back."

"Thank you." She shivered again.

"Here." Jace leaned over her and grabbed a fleece-lined sweatshirt from behind the console. He draped it around her shoulders and rubbed, trying to warm her. "How do you want to do this? Pull the boot or cut it?"

Meredith stared at his chest, but when she looked up, his face was close to hers. His features looked severe in the glare of the overhead light, but his soft gray eyes shone with caring. *What was the question?*

He leaned closer and barely brushed his lips over her forehead. "Be brave. I'm going to cut that boot off."

Meredith nodded.

These were her favorite riding boots, but she could replace them. Probably not a bad idea considering how worn they were. Her ankle was pounding now, and her foot had fallen asleep. That pins-and-needles prickling meant that the leather boot had grown really tight. "You might want to hurry."

"I know." Jace fished around in his toolbox in the back seat of his truck. He brandished a pair of what looked like huge, fat scissors and went to work, carefully cutting down the inseam of her leather boot.

He whistled. "Wow."

"What?"

"Your ankle looks pretty bad. It could be a sprain, but I better take you to the emergency for

X-rays. Just to be sure. Brace yourself, I'm going to pull the boot off."

She grabbed the handle above her and tensed. "Okay, ready."

Jace was careful and surprisingly gentle.

She felt a sharp twinge but got through it. She also felt humbled that he'd returned to her house. If he hadn't, she'd still be lying on that path trying to get her foot free.

"Why'd you come back?" Her voice came out barely above a whisper.

He pulled a couple of leaves from her hair, and then cupped her cheek. "I didn't like the way I left."

"I didn't like it, either," she said. "I'm sorry for—"

He put a finger to her lips. "We'll talk on the way. Swing your legs in and I'll close the door."

She did as he asked and watched as he walked around the front of the truck. It was true—they needed to talk. She shouldn't have said the things she had.

Once he was back in behind the wheel, she asked, "Would you mind stopping at the stable first? Bella needs to be unsaddled and given a quick rubdown so she doesn't get chilled. Plus, I'm going to need my purse."

"Of course." He reached his hand across the console for hers.

Meredith took it and held on tight. Time to be

honest with him instead of defensive. She wanted to go out with him and see where it went, but she was still afraid of a coworker or school counselor calling her on the carpet for a perceived ethical infraction.

The closest emergency room was almost forty-five minutes in either direction, so they'd have time enough to talk it all out. Letting out a sigh, she had a feeling this drive might prove to be one wild ride.

Jace took care of Bella. She'd been sweaty under the saddle blanket, so he'd rubbed her down with a towel from the tack room until she was dry. In the house, he grabbed an icepack and some ibuprofen before sweeping Meredith's phone into her purse that he found under the dining room table. He slipped back into his truck that he'd left running and handed the items to Meredith.

"Warm?"

"Yes, thank you." She'd turned down the heat but still snuggled into his thick sweatshirt. Her hair was all over the place, sticking to the inside of his truck. It made him chuckle.

"What?" Her eyes grew round.

He reached for her hair, plastered on the top of the cab. "Your hair is everywhere."

"I told you, it's a frizzy mess."

"I love it," he said as he pulled out of her driveway. "In fact, now that I think about it, when I first saw you lying on the trail with leaves in all that glorious red hair, you looked like some beautiful woodland creature."

One who'd lead him to the sweetest of deaths. He was ready to finally put to death the unfeeling, surface-level guy he'd been. When it came to Meredith, he wanted it all. Commitment had been something he'd avoided like the plague, but now he wanted a life with one woman as long as that woman was Meredith.

She laughed. "You probably say that to all the girls."

"No, Merry, I don't. Only you." He needed to break through her self-protective front once and for all, but driving to the emergency room wasn't exactly the place he envisioned telling her that he loved her.

He reached for her hand again, glad when she took it. Glancing at her, he noticed that although a smile teased her lips, her mouth looked tight. Her head rested against the seat and her eyes were closed. She was in pain from her ankle. He'd wait.

Still holding her hand, he gave it a light shake. "You okay?"

"I will be once the ibuprofen kicks in."

"Maybe we should pray."

"Please."

He'd never prayed with a woman before. Another first with Meredith. Taking a deep breath, he went for it. "Dear Lord, we ask that You touch

Meredith's ankle, give her peace and comfort. Amen."

She squeezed his hand. "Amen."

They had miles to go yet and they needed to talk, so he started off with an apology. "I'm sorry for earlier."

She turned her head to look at him with smudged-makeup-rimmed eyes that reminded him that she'd been crying. "Me, too. I shouldn't have said those things to you, Jace. You don't deserve them. I'm just scared."

"I know."

"I'd really like to go out with you."

He chuckled. "And a trip to the ER doesn't count."

"No, I guess it doesn't." She winced when they hit a bump in the road. "But I'm still concerned about any speculation of you as a client."

"You can prove that I was never your client, Merry. You didn't accept payment, for starters. And you didn't counsel me. You listened like a real friend. My best friend." Jace got brave and glanced at her again. "This isn't exactly the way I envisioned sharing this, but I love you, Meredith."

Her mouth fell slightly open in sweet surprise.

If he wasn't driving and she wasn't in pain, he'd have enjoyed kissing the surprise off her face. Instead, he grinned and focused back on the road. "I think I fell for you the moment I kissed you.

It felt like coming home and scared the daylights out of me."

"Jace—"

"You don't have to say anything. In fact, don't. Just know that I want more than just going out. I want a future together and I'll wait for as long as it takes to overcome your concerns."

She shifted her hand, threading her fingers through his. "I'd like that."

"Good." They'd have a fun story to tell their kids about how he'd professed his love on the way to the emergency room.

After several seconds of silence went by, she cleared her throat. "I have a lot of insecurities that won't go away overnight."

"I know. It'll give me incentive to prove that I'm not going anywhere. I'm in this for the long haul, not a shortcut. But you have to promise me to be careful. Always have your phone—" His voice grew thick with emotion. "Seeing you lying in the middle of that trail stopped my heart. I don't want to lose you, Merry. Not ever."

"I guess, we'll have to trust God with each other, then."

"Yeah." Jace brought her hand up to his lips and kissed it.

"Thank you, Jace."

"For what?"

"For building my arena, for supporting my program and being my friend, and now—for giving me the courage to love you out loud."

"I really like the sound of that."

She smiled then. "Me, too."

Jace saw things ahead he'd never pictured for himself before. A home, a family and a life worth living instead of just getting by. It had all started with a dark horse and the beautiful woman who owned her. God had used his construction skills to bring Jace to this place where God had not only gotten through, but also softened his heart.

Many times, Jace had heard the scripture about faith, hope and love, but now he understood it. Love truly was the greatest gift of all.

Epilogue

Four and a half months later...

Meredith peeked out her kitchen window and smiled as fat snowflakes fell gently from the sky. What a beautiful day for another date with Jace. Not too long ago, she had agreed to go public with dating Jace, and today they were headed into town for a Valentine's Day Festival complete with ice sculptures and a chocolate crawl. Fortunately, her ankle had healed, so she could tromp through the ample snow unhindered.

Since the RR Equine Therapy's grand opening event, she and Jace had kept a low profile. She'd gone to the Moore brothers' home for Sunday dinner after church a few times and Jace still came over to help with the horses. Tommy Tuesdays had wrapped up but Meredith knew she'd see the boy again come spring. Tommy was doing well, but his mom had asked if he might go on a trail ride when possible. And Meredith wouldn't refuse that request. In fact, she looked forward to it.

No one Meredith worked with, or the Rose River school counselor, had confronted her with any issues where Jace was concerned. His comment about her horses helping him hadn't been a big deal, nor had anyone made it one. She'd been the only one, but that was due to deeper fears that seemed far away now.

Hearing Jace's truck pull in, Meredith slipped on her coat, hat and mittens, and rushed out the door. "Hi."

Jace had gotten out and opened the passenger side door for her. "Ready to walk around and freeze?"

"I am. This will be fun and there's chocolate." Jace harrumphed.

After pulling away from her place, it didn't take long before they were parked on a side street of downtown Rose River. Meredith slipped out of the truck before Jace could open her door. "Thank you for doing this. It's very Valentines-y."

He grinned. "My mom loved this sort of thing. She dragged me and Jeremy to see the ice sculptures long ago, but we got into trouble for wrestling into one and breaking it."

Meredith chuckled then touched his arm, stalling him. "Will the memories bother you?"

"No. I welcome reminiscing as a way to honor my folks." He gave her that warm smile of his. "Plus, we're making new memories today."

"We are." Coming here together meant even

more, knowing he had a family history with the event.

Jace had been an anchor for her over the Christmas holiday, when he went with her to visit both her parents. They were definitely making memories together, like now, walking along a busy Main Street with people darting in and out of shops offering chocolate.

"Where do you want to start?" Jace asked.

"Let's look at the sculptures first, then we can warm up with hot chocolate somewhere."

"Lead on." Jace kept one hand in his coat pocket and the other wrapped around hers as they walked and walked, looking over one sculpture after another.

Meredith tugged him toward a raging bonfire in the park, where a hot chocolate stand had been set up and line had formed. "Let's warm up over there."

Jace grinned. "You're sure?"

She smiled back. "No doubts. That hot chocolate is calling my name."

They got in line and Jace turned to face Meredith.

"That's how I feel with you, you know. You called my name from the beginning and even though I was scared at first, I have no doubts." Then he dropped to one knee.

What was he doing? "Jace—"

The line suddenly fell apart into a circle as folks

watched them. Meredith recognized a few faces and then her heart skipped a few beats when it dawned on her what Jace was up to. *Right here, right now?*

"Merry—" He pulled a small, black velvet box from his coat pocket and flipped it open. "I thought this might make our Valentine's Day more memorable and it's the perfect day to ask. Meredith Lewis, I love you. Will you marry me?"

She'd held her breath, but the beauty of the ring made her gasp. A stunningly simple oval diamond was bezel-set in gold. It shimmered in the afternoon's light and then blurred as tears welled in her eyes.

Meredith gazed into Jace's dear face. The last few months, they hadn't shied away from revealing their fears, along with their hopes for the future. Jace hadn't scoffed at her request that they wait a little while before going out in public. Over and over, he'd proved his affection in the little things he did, like now, waiting patiently for her answer in front of a small crowd that waited, too.

Meredith slipped off her mitten and held out her left hand. "Yes, Jace Moore, I love you back and I will marry you."

The crowd cooed and clapped, and then fell back into line without them. And Meredith didn't care about hot chocolate anymore as Jace slid the ring onto her finger.

After tossing the box over his shoulder, he stood

and pulled off the other mitten, taking both her hands in his. "When?"

Meredith blinked. "When what?"

He shook his head, as if she should know better. "When do you want to get married?"

"I don't know." She laughed, pulling her left hand free. She wiggled her fingers, loving how the diamond seemed to catch fire from within. "Let's enjoy being engaged first."

Jace pulled her close. "We could have it this summer and use the arena. It's what brought us together."

"I didn't know you were so sentimental."

He dropped his forehead to hers. "I am when it comes to you."

Meredith basked in this feeling of being cherished. She'd do anything for Jace, but wasn't keen on the expense of a big wedding. Now that she was getting more referrals, she'd rather sink those funds into RR Equine Therapy.

And she needed to consider her parents. Did she really want her father walking her down the aisle? And her mom still wouldn't want to be in the same place with her father for long. A full-on wedding wasn't something she wanted to worry about.

"Or we could elope," she offered.

Jace grinned, looking entirely pleased with the idea. "Now, you're talking. But, I need my bothers there."

As she ran her fingers through his hair, she couldn't stop staring at her ring. "Maybe we can talk to the pastor and see what he thinks. We'll figure it out."

Jace rubbed his nose against hers. "I have no doubts."

Meredith shifted her gaze into his eyes. She'd spend the rest of her life with this man because he *was* the man for her. Jace had become her confidant, her most reliable volunteer and protector, and even her mentor in ways she was only beginning to realize as they drew closer to each other and God.

"I have no doubts," she whispered, knowing that was indeed true.

She might not be the most beautiful woman in the world, but that was okay. It didn't matter. The man she loved not only accepted her for who she was, but he also loved her because of who she was even with her red hair and freckles.

For that, she was truly grateful. And immensely blessed.

* * * * *

Dear Reader,

Thank you for reading my latest Love Inspired romance! I appreciate you picking up a copy and I hope you enjoyed Jace and Meredith's journey of healing from their painful pasts as they opened themselves up to risk falling in love.

For the sake of the story, I took fictional license with Meredith's ethical concerns, so any errors she made are my own.

I'm very fond of horses and am blessed with friends who have them, so I wanted to write a heroine with horses. The equine therapy premise morphed out of Jace's issues of not dealing with his grief. Like Meredith said in the book, fear is a powerful motivator that can keep us from living life to the fullest.

We all battle fear at one time or another, but remember that God tells us to fear not, for He is with us. He will guide us if we quiet our frazzled minds in order to hear His voice through His word. God's got this, and He's got us!

I love to hear from readers. Feel free to reach out to me through my website at jennamindel. com or my Facebook page at www.facebook.com/authorjennamindel/

Happy Valentine's Day!

With love,
Jenna

Get up to 4 Free Books!

We'll send you 2 free books from each series you try PLUS a free Mystery Gift.

FREE Value Over **$25**

Both the **Love Inspired®** and **Love Inspired® Suspense** series feature compelling novels filled with inspirational romance, faith, forgiveness and hope.

YES! Please send me 2 FREE novels from the Love Inspired or Love Inspired Suspense series and my FREE gift (gift is worth about $10 retail). After receiving them, if I don't wish to receive any more books, I can return the shipping statement marked "cancel." If I don't cancel, I will receive 6 brand-new Love Inspired Larger-Print books or Love Inspired Suspense Larger-Print books every month and be billed just $7.19 each in the U.S. or $7.99 each in Canada. That is a savings of 20% off the cover price. It's quite a bargain! Shipping and handling is just 50¢ per book in the U.S. and $1.25 per book in Canada.* I understand that accepting the 2 free books and gift places me under no obligation to buy anything. I can always return a shipment and cancel at any time by calling the number below. The free books and gift are mine to keep no matter what I decide.

Choose one:
- ☐ **Love Inspired Larger-Print** (122/322 BPA G36Y)
- ☐ **Love Inspired Suspense Larger-Print** (107/307 BPA G36Y)
- ☐ **Or Try Both!** (122/322 & 107/307 BPA G36Z)

Name (please print)

Address _____ Apt. #

City _____ State/Province _____ Zip/Postal Code

Email: Please check this box ☐ if you would like to receive newsletters and promotional emails from Harlequin Enterprises ULC and its affiliates. You can unsubscribe anytime.

Mail to the Harlequin Reader Service:
IN U.S.A.: P.O. Box 1341, Buffalo, NY 14240-8531
IN CANADA: P.O. Box 603, Fort Erie, Ontario L2A 5X3

Want to explore our other series or interested in ebooks? Visit www.ReaderService.com or call 1-800-873-8635.

LIRLIS25